SIMPLE THINGS

Stories, Poems, and Essays of Isolated Gratitude

I0557067

Edited by
Diana Kathryn Plopa
& Zachary B. Wolfe

For reprint permissions write to:

Pages Promotions, LLC

Birmingham, MI 48009

Info@PagesPromotions.com

© 2021 Pages Promotions, LLC
Edited by Diana Kathryn Plopa
Edited by Zachary B. Wolfe

Print ISBN: 978-1628282399

E-book ISBN: 978-1628282405

LOCCN: 2021909358

The Creative Light Writer's Guild
A Division of Pages Promotions, LLC

We believe a more harmonious and supportive society begins with literacy. We believe that a successful life begins with, and is enhanced by, the written word. We believe that not everyone is able or inclined to pick up trash by the side of the road or give blood or donate financially in order to contribute to the well-being of their community. We know there must be an alternative. We believe that alternative is the Power of The Pen!

One of the things that gives the pursuit of writing meaning is the impact our words have on the lives of others. What we write, whether real or imagined, can, and often does, spark tremendous connectivity with our readers. Words give others permission to feel, learn, and understand points of view or concepts that perhaps they would not have encountered, had they not picked up a book.

Works of charity, we believe, are essential to the empathetic, evolutionary path humanity must travel if it is going to sustain and prevail throughout the next seven generations, and beyond.

Without the goal of improving literacy standards the world over, our society is doomed to fail. An illiterate population hinders every aspect of a country's development... it's economy, agriculture, industry and manufacturing, arts, sciences, technology, and most importantly, governing. A society that lacks basic literacy skills is threatened by terrorists, despots, and, most tragically, apathy.

A Book's Purpose

This is a collection of short stories, poems, and anecdotal essays written by Indie Authors, as they reflect on their time in Isolation during the COVID-19 Pandemic of 2020. Each piece reflects a Moment of Gratitude from the authors' life: past, present, or anticipated future.

Proceeds from sales of this book support the World Literacy Foundation.

The World Literacy Foundation
Mission and Vision

"We strive to ensure that every young individual regardless of geographic location has the opportunity to acquire literacy skills to reach their full potential, succeed at school and beyond.   We envision a world in which every one of us can read and write, in which there is free access to education for all."

Table of Contents

Faith
Andrew Allen Smith

Agatha Fairchild was annoyed at the repeated knocking at her door. Agatha had very few visitors and wanted far fewer. Agatha surveyed her plush furnishings scattered throughout the spacious living room as she glided through towards the foyer. She noted with some annoyance that there was dust on some of the curios and made a note to herself that she would clean and polish those areas today after she dealt with whatever annoyance was coming her way. Agatha was a tall woman with crisp features that could easily have been mistaken for royalty and even aged seventy years she still radiated beauty. Agatha's silver hair was in a tight bun on top of her head and she checked the bun and tightened it as she reached the foyer and the offending door.

The door rapped again, and Agatha grimaced with the upcoming confrontation. The solid cherry door with ornate stained-glass windows swung open to reveal the secure black security door with bars and bulletproof glass that kept her quite safe from visitors and other people.

On the other side of the door stood a beautiful young woman in a mask with a young girl standing next to her, masked as well. The woman was thin and the child even thinner but not so much they looked ill. The two looked fit and tidy, almost as if they were ready to be in a fitness magazine advertisement. Both had striking blue eyes and the child was full of the youthful inquisitive look that Agatha used to see in children many years ago. The woman's eyes were frantic and puffy. She had obviously been crying over some unknown issue. Agatha instantly recognized them as her neighbors. The woman was Mary and the child was Faith.

"What do you want Mary?" Agatha asked.

"I'm sorry Agatha I know you hate visitors and you never really liked us, but I need your help."

Agatha raised an eyebrow then said, "You need my help?" The last word rung out and she emphasized it with sarcastic weight.

"Please Agatha I will beg if I have to, but I have just gotten the call and my son is in some trouble. I would like to take Faith, but I don't think I should. Please can you watch her for a short time while I get Franklin and bring him home."

Agatha had not lowered her eyebrow and simply asked, "You want me to watch a child in my home?"

"Please Agatha you know I just moved here and it's just me and the children. I have no one in the world but them. She is not a bother and she will listen to whatever you say."

"My home is not suitable for children," Agatha replied, "I don't think it is a good idea."

"Please Agatha," Mary asked again, "I will pay you all I can if you will just watch Faith for a short time; it shouldn't be very long. I'm sorry to be an imposition, but I have no one else to turn to."

"No, I don't think so," Agatha said as she began to close the door. As she looked down and the door closed, she saw Faith looking up at her. The innocence and inquisitive nature of her eyes said something that Mary never could have. She held the door for a moment. She stared at the child for a brief instant then looked back at Mary.

"Two hours," Agatha said, "and make no mistake she will have to wear that mask. I don't need any of this COVID-19 in my home." Agatha opened the security door.

Mary looked down at her daughter. "You listen to everything Agatha says."

"I will Mommy," said Faith, reaching up and holding her mother's hand for a moment. "It will be fine. Get Franklin, and make Franklin safe, and I will be waiting."

Mary looked up, tears in her eyes with her mask obviously damp from her crying, then spoke, "Thank you Agatha you don't know what this means."

"Yes, yes," Agatha said with obvious frustration. "Get your boy and get back here. I would hate to have to leave this ragamuffin on your front porch."

Mary looked at her daughter and smiled, but no one saw beneath the mask, she turned and walked to her waiting car. As Agatha and Faith watched from the security door, the pale silver Impala drove off, then Agatha turned and closed the ornate cherry door.

The door closed. Agatha looked down at the little girl. "How old are you?"

"I am almost seven years old ma'am," Faith replied looking up with those sparkling eyes.

"Well," Agatha said as she walked to the living room, "I do not have a TV in this room, and I suppose you have one of those smart phones to keep you busy." She turned; Faith had followed her diligently. "You can occupy yourself."

"No ma'am," Faith said, "I do not have a smart phone or a phone at all, Mommy says little girls don't need all that until they become older and more responsible. I have a book I can read while mommy is gone."

"Read huh?" Agatha replied, "So you know how to read."

"Yes ma'am," Faith said, "I love books. They show you new worlds and take you away from all the bad stuff."

"Indeed," Agatha said, "You seem much older than seven."

"Thank you, ma'am," Faith replied. "Mommy says reading has given me a good vocabulary."

"I will agree," Agatha replied, "Vocabulary is a big word for seven. What are you reading?"

"I am reading Frost right now, his poetry is very good," Faith said, her mask covering a smile that shone brightly in her eyes. "I hope to finish today."

"Really?" Agatha said obviously surprised at the reading level of a seven-year-old. She strained for a moment trying to remember how much she read when she was seven and could not recall. She looked at the little girl, standing, waiting for her every word. "This is my living room. The couch to the right or the chair to its left will be where you may sit. If I am not in the room you may remove the mask, but if you can see me the mask must be on, do you understand?"

"Of course, ma'am," Faith replied as she moved to the big armchair with red paisley fabric, "I will leave the mask on and read."

"Very good," Agatha said, "I noticed I need to clean and will be working, so amuse yourself but do not leave this room unless you have to go to the bathroom. If you do, the bathroom is in the center hall. Please wash your hands if you do anything and clean up after yourself."

"Yes, ma'am," Faith replied and literally jumped up into the chair holding her book, *The Poetry of Robert Frost*.

Agatha went to the kitchen and got a towel and some Pledge, she returned to the living room and Faith was paying close attention to the book in her hands as her eyes darted back and forth while she read. Her mask was tight on her face, a cute mask with small yellow butterflies on the print. Agatha went to a curio cabinet, sprayed Pledge on her cloth and began cleaning. She noticed Faith had put the book down and she looked to her, "You should keep reading."

"Ma'am, I was wondering if you wanted help?" Faith asked. "You have so many pretty cabinets. I bet it takes a long time to clean them all."

Agatha looked around the room, yes, it was a big job, but she rarely noticed as she did little else but eat, clean, and read. "Will you do a good job?" Agatha asked.

"Yes ma'am," Faith replied, "Mommy taught

me, and I will do very good for you."

Agatha considered, "Wait here, I will be a moment." Agatha went into the kitchen and got an additional towel, a small stool, and another can of Pledge. She considered for a moment and realized the child could overuse the Pledge, but it would not hurt. She returned and handed the linen cloth, Pledge, and small stool to Faith. "You start on this one over here," she showed the young girl to a cherry hutch with ornate claw work and deep engraved scrollwork.

"Yes, ma'am," Faith said and took the cloth and knelt on the floor. Agatha watched as she unfolded and refolded the cloth into a small square, then sprayed the cloth with Pledge. She then began to methodically clean the legs of the curio and Agatha almost smiled. She walked back to the curio she was working on and continued her cleaning. After about ten minutes Faith walked to her.

"What is it?" Agatha asked.

"Do you have some Q-Tips ma'am?" Faith asked.

"In the hall bathroom, there are Q-Tips on the top of each bathroom counter," Agatha said and the little girl nodded and walked down the hall. Agatha continued cleaning for several minutes and noticed the little girl was back. The girl was concentrating hard but Agatha could not tell at what, so she walked to the cabinet and looked as Faith was cleaning the scrollwork with a Q-Tip. She was being very meticulous as she sprayed the tip, then worked the Q-Tip through the scrollwork, wiped the Q-Tip off with the towel and continued again. Agatha watched in fascination as she finished and stood up.

"All done ma'am," Faith said, "Would you like me to start the next one?"

Agatha examined the child's work. She looked at the scrollwork and the crispness of it. She could not remember the last time the edges had been so clean. The entire curio cabinet now looked nearly new. She smiled a small smile and looked at the four cabinets in the room. One now shone above the rest, there were two yet to do while she was still working on hers.

"Are you sure you would like to keep working?" Agatha asked.

"Yes, ma'am," Faith said. "I like to help, and they are so pretty."

"Do you like the figurines?" Agatha asked.

Faith looked inside, and noted that all of the curio cabinets contained porcelain figurines. The one she was working on contained people, the others scenes, animals, and finally items.

"Yes ma'am, they are very pretty. The Snow White figurine is very pretty, but all of them are nice." The figurine was clean and showed the girl singing, her long dark hair flowing. The detail was amazing. The figure held an apple contemplating it with red ribbon in her hair and a flowing cape locked in an eternal wind.

"You know Snow White?" Agatha asked.

"Yes ma'am," Faith replied. "Her book is one of my favorites."

"Have you seen the movie?" Agatha asked.

"No ma'am." Faith said, "Mommy says we will someday, but it has been very busy, and we have had to move many times."

"I tell you what," Agatha said, her tone much softer, "If we finish up in time, we can watch the movie."

Faith's eyes twinkled, "Only if we finish though ma'am. We have to do our work to enjoy our play."

Agatha was near taken aback, "Yes child, we have to do our work to enjoy our play."

Faith moved to the second cabinet and began cleaning. She moved the stool as well and was incredibly detail oriented as she polished each inch of the curio cabinet.

Agatha finished hers and began on her second, as well. Smiling a little at the feeling of getting this chore done. "Faith," she said, "Why have you had to move so much?"

"Well, Father died. He was a doctor and died during the first part of the pandemic," Faith stated with more maturity than her years presented. "After Daddy died, Mommy lost her job. She tried really hard to get more and Daddy left us money, but it is tied up in something with bad men. I think they call it prorate."

"You mean probate?" Agatha asked.

"Yes ma'am, probate," Faith continued. "It will be okay, but Mommy is sad all the time, and Franklin is starting to work at the hospital now to help Mommy. Mommy is waiting tables. Sometimes the people who rent the houses to us don't want to rent to Mommy, so we have to move."

"But money is coming, right?" Agatha asked.

"Yes ma'am, but they don't know when," Faith said. "People have not been nice to Mommy. I try to help, but I am still little."

"Do you like your new house," Agatha asked. She looked back and Faith was cleaning the scrollwork and edging of the curio with a Q-Tip.

"Yes ma'am," Faith said, "But Mommy said she doesn't know if we will be able to stay."

"I see," Agatha said.

"How are you doing?" Agatha asked.

"I'm almost done." Faith said, "Can I help you now?"

"I am almost done too," Agatha replied. "What about your Grandma or Grandpa, can they help?"

"No ma'am, they died when Franklin was little." Faith said, "We are all alone."

"I see," Agatha said, "I did not think your Mommy was very old, but Franklin is older?"

"Yes," Faith replied, "Franklin is twenty years old. I was a good surprise Mommy says. She works so hard for Franklin and me."

"I see," Agatha said again.

Agatha stood, "I am done, are you?"

"Yes ma'am," Faith said.

"That just won't do. Call me Aggie or Aunt Aggie if you like, but ma'am is just not right. We can watch the movie in the sitting room. Are you hungry?"

"Yes ma'am," Faith said, "but I don't want to be a bother."

"Oh child, look at how pretty you made my cabinets," Agatha replied a small grin crossing her face as they surveyed their work, "It is the least I can do to thank you."

Faith smiled at the compliment and picked up her cloth, Pledge, and Q-Tips.

As Agatha did the same, she said, "Let's go make a snack." The two walked into the spacious kitchen and Agatha took the items from Faith and put them away. She took the rags and walked into a room behind the kitchen and returned with two aprons.

"What would you like to eat?" Agatha asked.

"Anything ma'am," Faith replied.

"Well, first, you and your Mom are not ill are you, or Franklin?" Agatha asked. "and you can call me Aggie or Aunt Aggie instead of ma'am."

"No, Aunt Aggie, we are all well, just Daddy got sick," Faith replied.

"Then take that mask off," Agatha said, "I am not sick either and my doctor insisted I got tested."

"Mommy had us tested too, after Daddy died," Faith said without a tear, "We were all healthy, Mommy said she did not want to take a chance of losing any of us. Mommy has been very sad lately." Faith took off her mask. Her features reminded Agatha of one of her figurines. "Do you have peanut butter?"

"Why yes, I do have peanut butter, I even have some nice strawberry jam, would you like that?"

"That would be awesome," Faith said as her eyes grew wide.

Agatha went to a cupboard and got out peanut better, then strawberry jam from the refrigerator. As she made the sandwich she asked, "You like Snow White?"

"Yes," Faith replied, "I like Snow White because she is a princess and isn't mean. People who are princesses should be nice to people, but Mommy said the people who we got houses from asked us to leave, why do they do that? Mommy says they have to make money, but Mommy will pay sometime, Mommy always writes checks, but she says you have to have money to write checks."

Agatha finished making a sandwich and cut all the crusts off the sides then slices it into four triangles. "That's true honey, you have to have money in the bank. I am sure it will work out soon."

"Mommy says the same, but I really don't want to move again," Faith replied, "Since Daddy died we have moved three times."

"That's very sad," Agatha replied as she cleaned up and put the sandwich on a small plate, "We will have to see what can be done. Should we watch the movie?"

"Only if you want to, Aunt Aggie," Faith replied, "I don't want to be a bother."

"It is no bother dear, it is one of my favorite stories," Agatha said. "Let's go in the den and watch the movie together. It will be our little party."

"I will finish my sandwich first," Faith said. "I don't want to make a mess."

Agatha thought for a moment about all the people who had visited her; of all of them, it was a child who had more manners than any. Even her family showed no care or remorse in visiting and leaving the house in a less than perfect state. They were all gone now, and she did not see them often. "Will you be messy?" Agatha asked after some thought.

"No, Aunt Aggie," Faith said, "I will not, but I don't want an accident to happen with all your pretty things."

"It's okay dear," Agatha said, "We will be just fine."

Agatha poured two small cups of milk and carried them into the den, followed by Faith holding her little plate. She made a spot on the plush blue couch for Faith and helped her set up a TV tray. She then set the drink on Faith's tray and put her drink on a coaster on the other side of the couch. She walked to a closed cabinet, opened it to show hundreds of movies. Agatha picked out a DVD, took it to a player and turned on a massive TV.

"Wow, that is a big TV," Faith said.

"I almost never use it," Agatha pondered, "I usually just read."

"Me too," Faith replied.

They both laughed as the movie came on. Faith's eyes got wide as the book opened and she smiled and said, "I know this part" as the pages turned. Moments later the animation started. The castle drew close and the evil queen came into view.

As the words "Rags cannot hide her gentle grace" were spoken Agatha looked at the young girl next to her and a tear formed in her eye.

Faith was mesmerized by the movie and the wishing well song played out before her eyes. She said not a word, but instead took small bites of her crustless sandwich, careful with each bite to not make any mess or drop a single crumb.

Agatha watched as the movie played out, as much interested in the little girl as the movie, but admiring the fantastic commitment and focus of the child. No interruptions or calls upon her, and instead she had finished her sandwich with a clean plate and finished her milk. On the screen before her, the dwarfs chased the evil queen in her haggard disguise, and as the lightning struck Faith jumped, and the vultures circled away slowly.

Still, Faith did not say a word. Tears formed as the music played and Snow White lay in her crystal coffin. Still the little girl was silent, each tear that fell was matched by Agatha's own. When the prince kissed Snow White and her eyes fluttered open, Faith gasped in joy and watched until she saw the words, "and they lived happily ever after."

As the movie closed Agatha stood and wiped her eyes with a silk kerchief. She walked to a cabinet and pulled another silk kerchief from a drawer and handed it to Faith.

"Thank you, Aunt Aggie," Faith said, "Thank you for everything. The movie was so good, and the sandwich was very good, it was the best day ever."

"What was your favorite part?" Agatha asked with a near childlike innocence in her words.

"It was all my favorite," Faith said, "but I would like to find the wishing well."

"Really?" Agatha asked, "What would you wish for?"

"I would wish for Daddy to be back, but if I couldn't have that, I would wish Mommy was happy again, and we could live happily ever after."

The doorbell rang.

"Do you think that is your mother?" Agatha asked, "Let's go see."

The two walked to the foyer and then to the front door. It had begun raining. Faith's mother stood at the front door alone, as rain fell on her.

Agatha opened the doors, "Come in child."

Mary stepped in tentatively, "Faith, where is your mask?"

"It is fine, we are not sick, we are just fine." Agatha said.

"No, no," Mary began, "She could put you at risk."

"True," Agatha replied, "But it is a risk I am willing to take. Come in and sit down."

"Aunt Aggie," Faith said, "May I go clean up my plate?"

"Oh yes, dear," Agatha replied, "I will help you in a moment."

"I can get it, and I will get your glass too." Faith said as she walked back to the den.

Agatha looked at Mary, "Sit with me for a moment." The two walked into the living room. As they sat down in two chairs Agatha said, "We need to talk. First how is your son?"

Mary was confused but stated, "He is fine, it was a mix up at the hospital, they confused him with someone else and I had to help him get it worked out. It is fine now. I am so sorry to be such an imposition." Mary's eyes teared again.

"I understand you are having some issue with the house?" Agatha asked and stated at the same time.

Mary looked at Faith as she straightened, "I see Faith has been talking to you."

"Faith is a very good young lady," Agatha said, "I did not expect that from a renter. It seems I have too many preconceived notions that I perhaps should not. It is not fair to you. I am sorry. I sat with a child in wide eyed wonderment tonight. She watched Snow White she says for the first time, and it showed. She had read the book but not seen the movie. As I talked to her I realized she is truly innocent but wise for her age in other ways. She reminded me of me as a little girl, and the special things my late husband and I had."

"I'm sorry Agatha, I did not know your husband..." Mary began.

"It is history, please set it aside," Agatha continued, "You have been taking some hard hits I understand."

"Yes ma'am," Mary said.

"I see where Faith gets her manners," Please, call me Agatha. "I am sorry this horrid COVID has been so hard on you, in so many ways. I have not helped. You see, I own the house you are renting, and I expressed concerns to my management company. That will stop. I know you have money coming, you will get through this, and it will be just fine."

"I don't know what to say," Mary replied, "I will be able to pay soon, as soon as the insurance pays."

"I know you will dear, and I know it has been hard," Agatha replied.

"Aunt Aggie," Faith had walked back into the room, "I cleaned my plate up. Do you want me to put the movie back where it belongs?"

"No dear," Agatha said, "I will take care of it. I am sure your mother wants to go home."

"Yes, Aunt Aggie," Faith said.

Faith put on her mask again, "Thank you Aunt Aggie for showing me your beautiful house and your movie."

"Oh dear, it was a pleasure having you here," Agatha said with sincerity as they walked to the door. She looked at Mary, "One more thing Mary. If it is okay, perhaps Faith can visit when you have to work."

Mary again looked at Agatha, "Are you sure?"

"Yes," Agatha said as she looked to the cherry door, "I had forgotten how some people in your life can make it better. Faith has shown me that."

Mary looked down at Faith, then back at Agatha, "Of course."

"Oh, and wait one moment," Agatha said as she walked to the back of the house. Mary and Faith waited by the door as Agatha returned with a box, she walked to her curio case and carefully removed the Snow White figurine. "Faith, I would like you to have this, for all your help today."

Faiths eyes lit up and Mary looked at the figurine, "Oh ma'am, I mean Agatha, that is far too much."

"Hush child," Agatha said and put the figurine in its original box. "Faith, do you think you can take care of this?"

"Yes, Aunt Aggie," Faith said, "I will cherish it always." Faith walked to Agatha and hugged her and did not let go for a moment. This time, Agatha held back a tear. As Faith and Mary walked out the door Agatha smiled for a moment. She closed the door behind them and walked back to the den, started the movie over and saw it through new eyes once more. Eyes that would see it now for the first time, every time.

Be Free
From Me
Trinity Slocum

My black faux leather boots sink slightly into the soft dirt as I trudge over to the stale red bench swing in my yard. It's been sitting there for ages, and the thought of swinging on it has never even crossed my mind. Leaves and twigs, among other things that may or may not be alive, are piled high on the wooden seat. I sweep them aside gently, trying not to disturb them too much, and sit delicately, unsure of the stability of the swing. As I draw in a deep breath, my throat tightens from the crisp wind and my bones relax as if time were slowing.

My mind is clear.

I start to sway slowly, smushing my toes into the ground and pressing my spine into the browning wooden back of the swing. I look out over the lawn through steady rocking and see the tired grey grass growing old with crunchy burnt patches, while the fresh moss is taking over. Throughout this war of mossy grass, hints of bright lime and tiger-striped maple leaves are dispersed sporadically. The teal long-needled pine trees sway thoughtlessly in the wind. I feel my heavy burgundy jacket warming my chest and arms, but my face feels the cool sensation of summer fading into an autumn breeze. The aroma of dirt and wilted leaves fills my nose. The chilly air leaves my hair refreshed with a smoky tinge from the bonfire down the road.

I leisurely rock in silence and peacefully listen to the crickets chirp under the brushing of branches in the breeze. The cars on the road behind my house glide swiftly over the asphalt making a humming sound as they pass me by, leaving a trail of harsh odors that waft into my clean fragrant yard. This stench leaves me feeling oily and light-headed causing me to smash my feet into the dirt and the wood to slam into the fleshy meat of my calves and come to a complete stop. I clench my fists into red balls of frustration so intensely my knuckles turn pale.

Why must humans ruin everything? All they do is start fights and replace beauty with decay.

I refuse to let this ruin my tranquility, so I begin to rock once more. It's not long before these irritations are replaced by the light airy smell of the dew evaporating off the leaves in equilibrium. The soft wind plucks the crackling burgundy paint from the seat like feathers from a bird. I hear acorns thudding through branches dropped by squeaky squirrels stocking up for the cold. The loud buzz of a cicada being re-birthed echoes in the distance.

The crusty chipped bench leaves my fingers raw to the touch like sandpaper, but I don't care. For the first time in months I can finally leave my worries, of politics and pandemics, behind and focus on the beauty right in front of me. I could sway here for hours in calming perpetuity. Loving, appreciating, and doing all the things humans are too busy to do.

As I slow to a stop and stand, rebalancing myself, the heels of my boots indent the dirt and I begin my slow stroll over the moist soil back to the house, reminding myself that I can always come back, whenever I so choose. I just have to choose it.

The Ways We Play
Andres Flores

We see each other day to day-
Our legs gallop on the breezing grass,
competing to be the fastest one alive.
Our feet strike a little ball into a goal,
while our chests gasp for any breath of air
as we dash past that one kid
driving his foot into ankles.
Our hands grip on monkey bars
with muscles gained from those twenty push-ups,
legs dangle as our fingertips embrace all the sweat.
Our legs squeak as we skid down the slide,
bright burn marks on our calves—
All this in forty minutes during lunch.

But now recess is no longer in our vocabulary,
For school, we use a six-inch screen to play
No more zooming outside for fifteen minutes,
just Zoom online,
Smoothly slide our thumbs up our phone
or bounce them round our keyboards,
our muscular arms only to provide for our thumbs,
while our bodies are paralyzed,
settled in a chair for the day.

If we compete and gallop on the grass,
it is not us—
just the virtual characters we control on an Xbox or PS4,
our thumbs wiggle the controller up and down.
Our swords strike a zombie in Minecraft,
Our characters slide under a wall in Call of Duty,
Our players grip their will on the basketball in 2K,
Our feet strike a soccer ball in FIFA—
all with the push of a button.

Yet now, in quarantine, the gang
still meets up every night
to talk on Facetime.
We use every app available without leaving the house.
I send them Tiktoks to watch,
they send memes from Instagram,
and we keep our streaks going on Snapchat.

Sure, life is different,
but we still make each other laugh.
And we see each other day to day.

My Home
Gina Killingbeck

I've always struggled with having a stable and loving home structure. As a child, I was always moving around hotels and houses, and people were always in and out of my life. This hasn't changed much during the pandemic—people continue their way through my life. But one person was always there for me, someone who always stuck around even through my hardest times. That person is my Grandmother.

My grandmother was always around when I was a kid. She'd take us out on summer trips to the zoo, and after saving for a few years we'd take a few trips to Disney World. She was always snapping photos of us at Christmas dinner, my little 4th of July birthday party—and any time she could, we would have a picture taken of us doing everyday tasks. Even today, without the family gatherings due to COVID, she has resorted to taking pictures of the autumn leaves this month, and pictures of us sleeping in the backseat on our road trips to nowhere.

My parents were never really a constant in my life. They still aren't. My mom has her own life in the city of Chicago, where she takes care of my little brother. My dad, on the other hand, has been taking care of his girlfriend's little boys, and together they have another little one on the way. Throughout my childhood, they always tended to miss my school performances and my award ceremonies. But my grandmother never missed one. She would always show up no matter how busy or how late she was; she was always there.

During 2020, I've had lots of moments of seclusion, and with seclusion I've had lots of time to think. I thought about things that truly make me happy, things I look forward to in life. The pandemic didn't affect my life too much. At most, it made me miss people I thought I wouldn't be missing. For example, it helped me build a better relationship with my brother before he went off to college this year, we spent a lot of time together, doing meaningless fast food runs and traveling to wherever we wanted. We would listen to music and dance until my phone died when we didn't have power for days. I'm grateful for these moments with him, because he is changing in his life and becoming an adult with his own choices and decisions. The lockdown helped me really think about my relationships with my friends and reevaluate if they were healthy or not. I was able to build myself back up from nothing; at the beginning of all of this I was at rock bottom.

In July, I made the choice to move out of my dad's house and move in with my grandparents. I was unsure at first, and for the first few weeks of early August, I felt like nothing was real. I was always on my feet, helping my brother move and getting ready for my final two years of high school. But my quality of life has gotten better. For the first time since I was little, I felt seen and I felt loved. Getting back on your feet is hard, but with the help of my grandmother, I was able to come home to a house full of people, a house where when I went in it wasn't cold and empty. Every night at 7 p.m., I get to eat a full and healthy dinner. I also get to learn about taxes and how to manage my money, things I had never had the opportunity to learn before.

In these past few months, I've learned more about life than I have in the last sixteen years. It's all thanks to this pandemic—without it I wouldn't have found my purpose. During the pandemic, I was able to spend more time indoors with my dad, and with that time I realized that we don't get along. I used to be a daddy's girl, but the differences in our opinions, and the way he made me feel I realized wasn't healthy and I needed to move on to be on my own. Life is bad sometimes, and right now everyone is experiencing that bad time, but there is always something important behind it. I'm eternally grateful for my grandmother's help. She helped me find a space that feels like my own, something I can be proud of and where I can express myself.

2020 has been a rollercoaster of emotions, that is for sure, but in this time I was able to build a strong bond with my grandmother, and we are able to see eye to eye.

An Artist Is Born
Alexandre Morrison

The rain came in droves
to wash away chalk drawings
I tentatively pulled out my stock-
dirty brushes, a loose assortment of pencils,
and cheap sets of paint without much previous
opportunity to be used
After so much destruction, I had to remember how to
create
So, leaving myself alone with my naked thoughts
and the empty canvas I had bought on sale,
 I saw my dreams completed
as if each brush stroke were a piece of a puzzle
or each subject a chapter to a book

And had I ever worked previously?
Without needing solace, had my work ever meant
anything?
I have never been gifted the time needed before
I'd never felt the delirium of completion in the past-
Only in 2020 would I have to step around my drying
compositions.
And only now could I put a price to my name and call
myself an artist.

What Is A Pandemic?
Shayla Bond

Sometimes self-care is listening to your favorite music at 3 A.M. on a Wednesday night. Thinking about all the things you're missing as you stare at the light on your ceiling. Making a pallet on the floor because it's the only sense of control you can find in the droning days once called a summer vacation. It's the vivid dreams (ones where someone from school you don't talk to is taking you on an adventure) your mind uses to keep you sane. Sometimes a pandemic is playing music too loud at 3 A.M. on a Wednesday night to keep anxious thoughts that scare you at bay, while you convince yourself that maybe you just like the song that much.

Sometimes a break from the stress is learning what products your Type 4 hair likes best on a Monday morning because school is no longer an option. Watching Criminal Minds, Avatar the Last Airbender, Legend of Korra, and badly produced rom-coms to laugh at while you follow a routine that seems never ending. An array of products frame the laptop on your desk. At first you had to remind yourself the order of each item: part hair, spray with water, apply cream, use oil, spread gel, twist, repeat. But eventually you find yourself getting lost in the 10th rerun of Spiderman into the Spiderverse. And every two weeks I have a standing date with myself, my hair, and whatever I can find on Netflix that won't be unbearable for the next few hours. Sometimes a pandemic is a taste of independence and self-love you haven't known before.

Sometimes father-daughter bonding is sitting on the porch people-watching and talking about absolutely nothing and everything from 7 P.M. to 9 P.M.

Maybe 10 P.M. on a weekend. Dad sharing songs he hasn't listened to in ages and me sharing music I've only just discovered. It's next door neighbors coming over just to get out of the house and saying things like, "I hope we can be like this with our kids someday." Some days you cry because it all hurts too much. And some days you laugh at the guy with no shirt or shoes with a Beats speaker on his shoulder; he always rounds the neighborhood on a bad day. Father-daughter bonding is watching your neighbor Trish tend to her plants and feed the squirrels. She likes to give out popsicles and fix loose screws on bikes for the kids in the neighborhood who are too young to wander the way they do. Sometimes a pandemic is talking to your dad from hours 7 P.M. to 9 P.M. about absolutely nothing and everything with light R&B playing as you wind down.

Sometimes family vacation is going to Boyne Mountain when you haven't been in years. It's scavenging for things you can still do amidst COVID-19. It's fishing even though you hate touching the fish after you've hooked them, but now you need to throw them back. We find ourselves racing a storm back to shore because we are too busy listening to our music to notice the clouds approaching from a distance. We drive the streets in rain sheets that are eager to drench us and find a Subway in what feels like the middle of nowhere. We stop for sandwiches there. Later we find a boardwalk for food and wander into a thrift shop. There I find a beautiful and yet simplistic necklace. The only charm is a pearl locked forever into a golden enclosure. The light catches it perfectly when I carry it outside of the glass box. Sometimes a pandemic is family vacation on the lake, on the boardwalk, and in a thrift store.

Sometimes family game night is just gibberish and drool dribbling down your face as you read off cards from a game. It's howling laughter well into the night because no one can quite get the words you've repeated at least three times and you're trying to swallow with your lips spread wayyy too far. It's being the best one at the game because you've been talking to your three-year old neighbor Leah who still has her baby accent and is forced to repeat the simplest of requests constantly. It's trying to understand your sister's boyfriend's Detroit accent when he can't even speak correctly with the hard plastic pulling his face into a terrifying smile. Sometimes a pandemic reminds you it's not evil to learn to smile in a crisis.

Sometimes the Fourth of July celebration is dancing in the dark to music you've known since before you could speak. After shooting the few fireworks we have left over from weeks of boredom, my brother and I grab a speaker from the inside of the house. The night still feels young and soon we're dancing. I'm teaching him to do the Kid-N-Play dance to the rhythm of Poison by BDV. Our laughter, ringing in the still air between distant booms, is enough to attract a neighbor who has just sent the last of her guests home. She comes to our porch and I drag her into our circle of happiness and bad dancing.

Sometimes the Fourth of July brings your sister home in the name of family, and the commotion outside of the house leads her to join your private party. It makes her shake her head and scrunch up her nose at the next song in your dad's playlist until she talks her way into dee-jaying. For an hour the four of us sing to each other and dance away everything wrong with the world.

Sometimes the Fourth of July helps you find your footing when you're barefoot in the grass belting Electric Relaxation by A Tribe Called Quest. Surprising your dad when he realizes you know more words than he does. Sometimes even your mom comes outside after working hours much too long and makes it a party of five. We teach each other new dances; my sister tells us about what she calls the Detroit shuffle. Later I show my family this new footwork move I've been doing for weeks. Midsummer mosquitoes threaten us with a promise of regret in the morning when their injected serum grows into a red itchy bump, but we dance on. And if you're dorky enough, the slap you give to a mosquito on your shoulder becomes a dance move.

When we take to slow dancing, my dad twirls me around on his finger as we two-step well into the night. And when all of us finally decide we've had enough of the bugs and bats dancing with us, and the soles of our feet ache, we slowly migrate back inside at 3:32 A.M. Sometimes in a pandemic the end of the night is bittersweet, but you know everything will be okay because you feel so at home and you can't think of a single way the night could have been better.

Sometimes in a pandemic, you're not so afraid.

Metaplasia Through Infliction
Nicholas Wheeler

We gather at wells of liquid truth
To touch each other
Feel the endorphins in our blood
Blood like constellations gleaming upon
The white canvas of ship sails
We are bound by the creaking timbers
That built vessels
We sway to the dark heart of the ocean
And drift further from insanity
Centuries of shared soil
Means shared steps
Original matter holds significance over us
For the world we live in has bestowed upon us the
greatest truth of all;
The inclination to find solace in others
The undeniable bond to chemically induced sympathy

L'Dor V'Dor
(From Generation to Generation)
A Zachary Blake Legal Thriller Prequel
Mark M. Bello

Prologue: 1990

Max Lewin studied his inquisitive grandson on the eve of the boy's Bar Mitzvah. The family had just attended a Kabbalat Shabbat service at the synagogue, welcoming the arrival of Shabbat.

Because he was the Bar Mitzvah boy, Max's grandson, Zachary, sat on the bimah for the service. Zachary was honored to chant the evening service, the prayer over the wine (he was permitted to take a sip!), and sing Shalom Aleichem, praising peace, the women of the house, and thanking G-d for allowing their family to reach this day. After the joyful service, the family walked back to Bubbe and Zayde's house on Pennington, a couple of blocks from Beth Abraham Synagogue, the Shul, Max called it, located on Seven Mile Road in northwest Detroit

When they arrived at Bubbe and Zayde's house, the women quickly retired to the kitchen. Before long, the family was seated at a mammoth dining room table, enjoying the traditional Shabbat dinner, the Jewish excuse to over-eat. When dinner was over, the women stayed in the dining room and kitchen, clearing the table and washing the dishes. The younger children ran to the basement where Bubbe and Zayde kept all the toys. The men went outside for a 'puff' as Zachary's father referred to smoking cigars. Max and Zachary ventured into and were left alone in the old man's study.

Overpacked bookshelves lined the walls. An ornate wooden desk sat in the middle of the room, with an oversized executive chair at the front, and two more swivel chairs on the opposite side. Max walked around the desk and sat down in the executive chair. He held his hand out across the desk, motioning for his grandson to sit in one of the swivel chairs opposite him. Zachary did as he was gestured. He sat down and waited, silently demanding his grandfather keep his promise. Tonight, on the eve of his Bar Mitzvah, Max would tell him the infamous story. Zack's parents gave permission once Zack became a man. Zie gezunt— tonight was the night.

This was not an easy repetition for Max. His voyage to Detroit was not planned. He had been happy and prosperous in the old country. He had a good business, was relatively well off, and enjoyed life in Warsaw. That is, until the Nazis invaded Poland and hell on earth began, especially for the Polish Jewish population. Prior to the war, there were 3,500,000 Jews living in Poland, mainly in the cities. Jews were a minority, making up about 10% of the general population. At the end of the war and the subsequent Soviet invasion, only 500,000 Jews were left. 3,000,000 Polish Jews perished in the Holocaust, roughly half of all Jews killed during the Shoah.

Max Lewenstein, now known as Max Lewin, was one of those Jews caught up in the onslaught. Max was captured, tortured, and sent to Auschwitz to die. Miraculously, he didn't die. Many students of the Holocaust ask why the Jews were so passive, so willing to lay down their arms, do what the Nazis demanded, and willingly walk to their deaths in prison camp gas chambers.

It is certainly true that millions of Jews were loaded on overcrowded, filthy, rail cars, for transport to unknown destinations. Thousands of able-bodied Jews worked in forced labor camps, while millions more wasted away, were gassed, or brutally murdered in concentration camps. These people were stripped of weapons, tortured, exposed to disease or disease experimentation, or literally starved to death. Most were unaware that death awaited them when gas chamber doors closed and gas, rather than water, filled the chambers. By then, it was too late. And those who did resist were usually shot to death by their captors. Worse, if a Jew successfully resisted, and harmed or killed a Nazi, not only would the Jew be executed, but the Nazis would hunt down his entire family and execute them, as well.

Still, Jews stubbornly resisted, in many other ways. Poets and singers would entertain fellow prisoners. Underground newspapers were printed, at great risk to those who participated in their publication. Furthermore, while educating children or praying were verboten, makeshift schools were created and camp residents held 'synagogue" services with surprising regularity. Observing kashrut, Jewish dietary laws, was also forbidden and subject to severe punishment, but many observant Jews ignored these edicts, also a risky endeavor.

While it may have been the exception rather than the rule, the Jewish community did what it could, when it could, to defy Nazi tyranny. When Jewish slave labor was used to create items for the Nazi war effort, these items, materials or weapons, would often malfunction or completely fail, due to deliberate sabotage or poor workmanship.

And, contrary to the myth of little or no resistance, there was, indeed, verified armed resistance to the Holocaust, in ghettos and concentration camps. The infamous Warsaw Ghetto uprising is the most famous example of 'ghetto' resistance, and there were also camp explosions and escapes in Treblinka, Sobibor, and Auschwitz.

The reason Max was sitting in his own home, surrounded by family, enjoying his comfortable study, in the company of his beloved and impatient grandson, was that he, Max, was one such example of Jewish resistance. Did Max survive because he was brave? Perhaps. Lucky? Absolutely! Stupid? Undoubtedly so. But the number one reason Max sat in front of young Zachary Blake on the eve of the boy's Bar Mitzvah was Max's stubborn refusal to give up or give in.

The old man glared over the desk at the defiant youngster. *He'd wait me out if his parents would let him. A promise is a promise, but is he ready for such a tale? I've only shared this story with a select few, and only for the purpose of Holocaust remembrance. This is my precious boychik, my grandson. Will this scar him going forward? Oy vey!*

Zachary's voice broke the long silence and startled his grandfather from his thoughts.

"Zayde? You promised! You promised to tell me the story when I became a man. I led the service this evening. Today is my thirteenth birthday. According to Jewish law—I am a man now." The boy folded his arms across his chest. He was stubborn, determined, like his grandfather.

"Oh, Zachary, my beautiful boy! Yes, today, you are a man. This is not an easy story to tell or to hear, but a promise is a promise. It is okay with your mom and dad, yes?"

"Yes, Zayde. They know about the story and your promise. And they want me to hear the story direct from the horse's mouth."

"So now I am a horse? A horse is not kosher!"

Zack laughed. Zayde is so funny, he sighed. "Very funny. You know what I meant. Stop stalling and tell me the story."

"Such a stubborn yingele! Okay, okay, young man, here is your story…"

Chapter One: 1939 to 1943—The Ghetto

"I was born and raised in the Jewish section of Warsaw, Poland. Before the war, Warsaw was a wonderful place to be Jewish. Life was very much like it is here in America, where a Jew is free to be a Jew. Do you know what I mean?" Zayde Max began his story.

"You had synagogues, kosher markets and restaurants, the freedom to do and be what you want?" The boy was wise beyond his years.

"Yes, it was like that, and more. The Jews were a large percentage of the population of Warsaw. Can you imagine, Zachary? We lived in Jewish neighborhoods and almost everyone one out you see on the street is Jewish? It was almost like being in Eretz Yisroel. We were the largest Jewish population in Europe, second largest in the world!"

"What was the first?" The boy wondered.

"New York City, my son."

"Not Israel?"

"Not in those times. Shall I continue?"

"Please, Zayde, yes, continue. I want to hear the whole story."

Max Lewin sighed. *Here goes...*

On September 1, 1939, Germany invaded Poland. In Warsaw, where Max Lewenstein lived and owned his bedding factory, the bombardment was devastating and non-stop. It took only twenty-nine days for Poland to surrender to the Nazis and for German troops to march into and occupy Warsaw.

A week later, the Judenrat was established and Jews were forced to segregate, report in, identify themselves as Jews, and wear white armbands with blue Stars of David. Jewish schools were closed. Jewish property and wealth were confiscated, and Jews were forced into labor. Life was terrible, but the Jews persisted as best they could. A year later, the Nazis established the Warsaw Ghetto.

The Ghetto order required all Jews to move into a small area of Warsaw. Then the Nazis came in and sealed the area off from the rest of the city. The Germans built a ten-foot-high wall topped with barbed wire around the Ghetto. Jews were trapped, ordered to stay in the Ghetto upon penalty of death. Guards were posted to help prevent Jews from leaving the Ghetto. The Nazis moved Jews in from other towns and cities around the country. Soon, in an area about the size of a square mile, there were 400,000 Jews living in that small place. Every building, every room, was packed with Jews.

Word of the Warsaw Ghetto spread to the worldwide Jewish community. Jewish organizations attempted to provide needed assistance, but the Nazis made this very difficult. People were dying, every day, from starvation, exposure to extreme weather conditions, or disease. There was so little food, even children were starved to death. What little food there was had to be smuggled into the Ghetto by brave Jewish and religious aid workers from other religions.

For almost three years, every day, thousands of Jews were taken from the Ghetto and sent to death camps, primarily the one called Treblinka. Those who resisted were killed on the spot, almost 50,000 Jewish citizens.

In the Spring, 1943, the Nazis decided to clear out the Ghetto, murder those who resisted, and send the rest to camps. Max and others organized, resisted, armed, and barricaded themselves, killing a number of Nazi SS units. The Warsaw Ghetto uprising lasted for four weeks. Seven thousand Jews died in those four weeks. Those who were left, Max included, were rounded up by the Nazis and sent to concentration camps.

Chapter 2: The Capture—1943

Colonel Karl Von Stein strutted back and forth, surveying the terrified, shivering group standing before him. Despite frigid temperatures, the captives were clad in undergarments; their hands were bound; feet were in chains. Von Stein was flanked by several German soldiers, all holding submachine guns, salivating for an opportunity to kill a few Jews and impress their commander.

Von Stein hailed from a long line of proud German military types. His father was also a colonel, and his grandfather on his mother's side was a rather famous general, prominent during WW I. On this cold night, Von Stein stood before his scantily clad audience, charged with processing the group into the camp. He believed this assignment was beneath him. Others were in charge of rounding up this scum, interrogating them, and killing those who were considered potential rabble-rousers. Others were assigned and stationed at the front, commanding their own divisions. As Von Stein was surveying and beginning what he considered a 'babysitting assignment,' other men of his rank and stature were leading brave men into battle, enjoying the honor and glory bestowed only upon 'war heroes.'

All things considered, though, Von Stein was a loyal and devoted Nazi. He had a job to do and he would do it, ruthlessly and efficiently. He would follow orders and adhere to the chain of command. He turned to his assistant, Schultz, a diminutive figure who defied the Aryan myth. His size and looks assured that the only role in the chain of command he would ever serve was that of 'assistant.' As a result, Schultz had a massive chip on his shoulder and was eager to take out his frustrations on some helpless, bound and chained, Jews.

"Do you have their identification papers?" Von Stein addressed Schultz.

This was more command than request, and Schultz immediately handed a stack of papers to his commander. Von Stein began to leaf through them, casually and carelessly. He quickly concluded this was a valueless group. Many were woman and children. None of the men served in the military; they were mostly shopkeepers, tailors, bookkeepers, or farmers. No one in the group could possibly possess information important enough to enable Von Stein to impress his superiors.

Von Stein was about to discard the papers in disgust, when his attention was drawn to one man, the owner of a bedding factory in Warsaw. According to this man's dossier, in its heyday, the factory employed over 1000 people. The Nazis recently entered the factory, pulled most of its employees off the floor, and dragged them off in chains. The owner was not in the factory at the time of these arrests. Instead, this man was arrested when Nazi stormtroopers put down the Ghetto uprising. Was he involved in the uprising? The planning of the uprising? Is he a potential leader of this helpless swine?

"Max Lewenstein! Jewish Swine! Step Forward, schnell!"

No one spoke—no one moved. Von Stein again surveyed the shivering group standing before him. He walked up to a small boy, perhaps eleven or twelve years old, and violently yanked him out of line. He turned the boy around to face his countrymen, pulled out a pistol, and placed the muzzle against the child's left temple.

"Max Lewenstein! Jewish Swine! Step Forward, schnell!" he repeated, pulling back the hammer on the pistol.

"Here." A man to the far right of the colonel stumbled forward as best his chains would allow. He stood at attention. Von Stein walked up to him, surprised he hadn't noticed him before. He was a good-looking man (for a Jew), with a square jaw, dark brown hair, greying at the temples. He was well-built and surprisingly tall (for a Jew), almost six feet, without shoes.

"You are Lewenstein?" Von Stein growled, releasing the boy and shoving him back toward the line.

"Yes." The man whispered. The boy fell face first into the mud and began to cry. Lewenstein bent over and hauled the boy to his feet with one arm and a stern look, willing him to be silent. Somehow, the boy understood the message and acquiesced.

"Why didn't you reply the first time?"

"I didn't hear you the first time, Colonel. I apologize. I'm hard of hearing." Lewenstein lied, face-to-face, eye-to-eye with his captor.

"Defective, like most Jews, eh? Did I grant you permission to look at me?" Von Stein snarled. He grabbed a submachine gun from one of his soldiers and butted Lewenstein in the head. The man stumbled backward, in obvious pain, but did not fall. He regained his balance, resumed his position at attention, and stood in front of Von Stein. This time, he stared at the ground.

"What do you do in Warsaw, Jew?" Von Stein demanded. He knew what Lewenstein did in Warsaw, but he wanted to see if this Jew scum would be truthful.

"I own a factory," Lewenstein admitted, continuing to stare at the ground.

Von Stein laughed, heartily. "You mean, you used to own a factory?"

"Yes, sir." Lewenstein grumbled.

"You are used to telling people what to do, yes?"

"If you mean those who worked in the factory, yes."

"And the same in the Ghetto, no?"

"I don't understand, sir."

"You were part of the Ghetto uprising. Don't bother to deny it."

"If you are ordering me not to deny it, Colonel, I will not deny it, but I do not know what you are referring to."

"If this group of worthless trash wants to live through this experience, they will need someone to speak for them and take responsibility. Will that be you?"

"If that is what you require, Colonel, yes."

"And you understand the chain of command?"

"Sir?"

"Defy me and you die, along with every other piece of Jewish filth in this group. Do you now understand the chain of command?"

"Yes, Colonel."

"Defy any of my men and all of you die, understand?"

"Yes, Colonel."

Suddenly, there was some commotion down the line, a rattling of chains. A woman managed to free herself. She turned and ran up the hill. In short order, Nazi soldiers chased her down, captured, re-chained, and returned her to Von Stein. She fell to her knees before the colonel, pleading for mercy. Von Stein signaled his troops and they began to punch and kick the woman, causing her to slink into the mud, screaming in pain.

Max was beside himself, but he did not dare intervene. After Von Stein's men kicked and beat the woman senseless, the colonel strolled over to her fallen body, face down in the mud, pulled out his pistol, and shot her in the head. Max did not know the woman, and she had brought this upon herself with her foolish attempt to run. Perhaps she decided immediate death was better than the fate awaiting the rest of the group.

"Why did you have to kill her?"

The question was asked by the boy who had been pulled out of line and threatened earlier. Von Stein turned, aimed the pistol, and shot the boy between the eyes.

"Anyone else have a question?" he snapped.

No one spoke. Max wasn't certain anyone even breathed at that moment. Lesson learned.

"This is where you come in, Lewenswine." Von Stein deliberately mispronounced Max's name. He smirked, amused at his own play on words. We could have prevented the deaths of two able-bodied workers, if someone had intervened and prevented their insubordination. Understood, Lewenswine?"

"Understood, sir."

"Understood by all?" Von Stein glared up and down the line. No one uttered a word.

"Understood by all?" Von Stein repeated.

Max waved his arm upward, imploring the group to reply.

"Yes, sir," a few replied.

"I can't hear you." Von Stein cupped his hand to

his ear. Max raised his arm a second time.

"Yes, sir," came the loud reply.

Chapter 3: The Camp—1943

Witnessing the old-blooded murder of a woman and a child was a sure-fire method to obtain the cooperation of the surviving members of the captives. Max assumed 'command' as ordered by Von Stein. The entire group of men, women, and children, were loaded onto a train, jammed into a single car. The car was already occupied by another fifty or so prisoners, and reeked of human vomit, feces, and urine. A bucket sat in the corner, apparently to serve as the only available 'toilet'.

People were jammed so tightly into the train car, they could not sit. They had to stand for the entire train ride to hell. Several passed out from exhaustion or the smell; others died in a standing position. Ten hours later, the train arrived at its destination. It pulled to a stop; the doors opened to sunlight, causing all to squint, blinded by the sudden burst of light.

A ramp was lowered, and the group was ordered to disembark from the car. Max was one of the first to exit—he looked left, then right, and saw that the train contained well over twenty cars, filled with hundreds of prisoners, bound and chained, in similar fashion to his group. All Jewish? He wondered.

Prisoners of both sexes, all ages, in good, fair, and poor condition stood on the ground, looking around, in various states of confusion and terror. Some prisoners fell to the ground, moaning in agony, others fell to the ground dead. The able-bodied were ordered to pick up the remains of those who perished, so Max and others began to comply with the orders of their captors. Max thought of Passover and Jewish slaves—manhandled and beaten by their Egyptian taskmasters. A large pit had been pre-dug. Several emaciated bodies already lay in plain sight, and Max and his men were ordered to toss bodies on top of those already in the pit. The sights and sounds of body after body, landing on another, over and over, was something Max would never forget.

As he turned to retrieve another body, Max glanced at the camp entrance, where the train came through. A gate marked the entrance. The sign read: "Arbeit macht frei" a German phrase that mean "work sets you free." The sign was a cruel taunt, as this was certainly not a place where work set a person free. There was no freedom, no matter how hard a prisoner worked, unless the prisoner escaped or was liberated.

Max and the rest had arrived at Auschwitz, the infamous Nazi death camp. Originally, Auschwitz was designed as a camp for Polish political prisoners, including Jews. However, it soon became a death camp, a place where Jews, by the thousands, were slaughtered, gassed, and tossed into pits like the one Max had just deposited his deceased fellow travelers. Max determined, then and there, that he would escape from this horrible place, or die in the attempt.

****

Shortly after his arrival at the death camp, Max Lewenstein was dragged at gunpoint into the office of the commandant. Nazi soldiers yanked him this way and that, violently depositing him into a hard, wooden chair at the side of a small desk. A photograph of Adolf Hitler in full military uniform adorned the wall behind the desk. A name plaque placed on the surface of the desk read "Commandant Helmut Kellermann". The commandant held the highest rank in the camp and was its ultimate authority. *What does he want with me?* Max wondered.

After a short wait under guard at gunpoint, Max watched the commandant saunter into the small office. Max was yanked to his feet by his captors and compelled to show proper respect to the commandant. His captors clicked their heels loudly, extended their arms and hands upward and shouted: "Heil Hitler."

"Heil Hitler," Kellermann huffed, with a half-hearted hand salute and far less verbal enthusiasm. He sat down, pointed to the seat, and the soldiers pushed and shoved Max into the seat.

"I wish to make clear certain rules…" Kellermann began, in German. "Sprichst du Deutsch?"

"No," Max replied, in Polish.

"English?"

"No," Max replied, again, in Polish.

"You don't speak English at all, stupid Jew?"

"A little," Max replied, in English. In truth, Max did speak English. He also spoke fluent Yiddish, a language very similar to German. As such, he understood German very well, but he was not going to make things easy for this asshole.

"As I said earlier, I wish to make clear…"

"Certain rules," Max interrupted, in broken English. "I hear you the first time."

Kellermann, for some unknown reason, chose to ignore Max's insubordination.

"Yes, certain rules, danke schon," Kellermann smiled, despite himself.

"And they are?" Max wondered out loud.

"And they are what?" a confused Kellermann retorted.

"These rules?"

"These rules, what?"

"What are these rules?" Max spelled it out for him, fearing retribution could come at any moment.

"The rules, yes, the rules. Stop speaking, Jew, when I am speaking. The first rule you need to understand is that you will not speak while I am speaking."

"Understood, Herr Commandant," Max conceded.

"And you will follow the orders given by me and by these guards at all times."

"Understood. Anything else?"

"You will be responsible for the behavior of everyone in the camp. If anyone disobeys in any way, that person and you will be punished."

"Understood."

"Your job is to follow all commands and orders and make sure all new prisoners follow commands and orders."

"Understood."

"Rule number three: No one, and I mean no one escapes from this camp. If someone tries, he will be shot, as will many others, in order to teach a lesson no one will never forget. If you and the others follow orders and work hard, maybe you will survive this place."

"Understood."

"I would rather kill people than spend any time or energy hunting down prisoners who attempt to escape. Is that understood?"

"Understood." If Max had any doubts about attempting to escape, this conversation alleviated them. He would not end up like the men and women in the pit, naked, emaciated, humiliated. He would escape or die trying. Max wanted to spit in Kellermann's face and tell him he felt obligated to try to escape. It was his duty to buck the authority of those who commanded the camp. Wisely, he held his saliva and his tongue. He decided to bide his time, cautiously determined to hatch an escape plan.

"Besides, swine, this camp has been built to hold prisoners. It was designed by the Fuhrer himself, with security measures that inferior men like yourself would not understand. It would be suicide to attempt an escape," Kellermann warned.

"Thanks for the warning," Max uttered.

"I don't like your tone…" Kellermann glanced down at the papers on the desk in front of him. He'd forgotten Max's name… "Lewenstein," he read from the papers, finishing the statement.

"I meant no tone, Commander," Max retorted, with deference.

"If you and your people behave and work hard, we will get along fine, and everyone may survive the war."

Sure, sir, I believe that… "I plan to behave and work hard, sir," he lied. "And I will do my best to make sure the others understand your message and your rules."

"That is all, then, take him to his quarters."

More "Heil Hitlers" followed. Max was yanked to his feet and dragged to his quarters. "Quarters" were over-crowded, small farmhouse-looking buildings, with two-tier bunk beds stacked within two inches of each other. A wooden embankment with five holes punched out sat in the corner of the building. The horrendous stench confirmed that these were toilets for use by everyone in the building. The prisoners were required to clean the latrines—eventually, everyone would get a turn.

That evening, Max lay in his bunk. The hard surface was keeping him awake—by now, he was used to discomfort, but he had a lot on his mind. What a dreadful place. I cannot and will not be responsible for everyone in these quarters. I will not spend a moment more in this place than is absolutely necessary. I must plan my escape.

Chapter 3: The Escape—1944

Six months later, battered, bruised, famished and exhausted, Max Lewenstein continued to plot his escape. He witnessed several attempts, foiled by guards in the watchtowers or electrified barbed wire fencing. He also witnessed Nazi retribution. For each escape attempt, ten prisoners were forced to starve. Max, himself, was brutally tortured as a consequence of one of the attempts.

Max was buoyed by the brave attempts of his comrades, and by the fact that Nazi revenge tactics, cruel as they were, had yet to result in anyone's death. Everything changed one evening, when Max learned Commandant Kellermann designated Jules Shulman (one of Max's bunkmates) as someone to be executed as retribution for the inmates last escape attempt. Kellerman decided to deliver a clear message that escape attempts would be met with the ultimate punishment.

The vast majority of prisoners were Jewish. A chosen few, with privileges, were Christian Poles, most of whom had no love for Jews. In fact, Christian prisoners almost uniformly blamed Jewish prisoners for their captivity in these deplorable conditions. They resented being treated like their "Jewish scum" neighbors. Despite this fact, from the day he was brought to the camp, Max cultivated relationships with his fellow Christian prisoners. Slowly, surely, the Christian men began to like and respect Max, despite his Jewishness. One of these Christians was Lech Kozlokowski, whose status as a master mechanic and Christian provided him access, from time to time, to SS vehicles. Max, because of his bedding experience, worked in the prison tailor and laundry shop, where prisoners repaired or made, among other things, SS officer uniforms.

Max and Lech devised a plan. Max would declare a few uniforms unrepairable, repair them, stash them, and wait for the opportunity to disguise themselves as SS officers. Kozlowkowski would steal the SS car, and off they would go. To spare those who remained behind from Nazi retribution, Max recruited

Shulman and two more prisoners, a Christian minister, and a semi-famous Jewish former athlete. The men would leave the camp as a five-person garbage disposal unit. If all five disappeared, Max decided, an SS officer would be held responsible rather than the prisoners left behind. The men swore to commit suicide by shooting each other if they were caught.

On garbage day, the men pushed a heavy garbage dumpster cart through an inner camp gate. Once clear, Kozlowkowski separated from the group to commandeer a vehicle from the repair shop. The other four men slithered through a laundry chute and into the laundry and tailor shop, where they recovered their stashed SS uniforms and some make-shift weapons.

When they exited the shop on the side opposite the gate, Kozlowkowski was waiting for them in a Mercedes Benz 770 W150, a revised version of the W07, with a top speed over 100 miles per hour. Max wondered, silently, how Kozlowkowski could get his hands on such a vehicle. He flashed a sinister smile at Lech and handed him an SS officer uniform. If he was going to drive the car, he needed to look the part.

Lech quickly donned the uniform, all five men entered the vehicle, and Kozlowkowski took off for the main gate. The men shouted "Heil Hitler" to prisoners and SS officers along the way. No one seemed to suspect they were imposters driving in a stolen vehicle. However, their plan was almost derailed when they approached the main gate, their final barrier to freedom, and it remained closed. At 80 meters, then 60, the gate remained closed. The men began to sweat, Lech began to panic. They would soon be directly under the "Arbeit macht frei" sign.

"We have twenty meters to go and the gate is still closed," he cried.

What happened next is legendary in the anals of Auschwitz history, and has made Max Lewenstein (aka Max Lewin) and his crew famous in Holocaust survivor lore. With all the courage he could muster, Max stuck his head out the passenger side window and yelled "Open the gate, you idiots!" in perfect German. "I've got to get this car to Himmler."

The stunned gatekeepers rushed to open the gate and the five men drove through it to freedom and into the history books. This was one of the most daring, dangerous, talked about, and legendary escapes in Auschwitz history. Once free, the five men went their separate ways. Max never heard from Kozlowkowski, Shulman, or the Christian preacher again. He hoped they escaped without incident and lived long and happy lives.

In the late-1950s, Max received a telegram from, Rudolph (Rudy) Roth, the former Jewish athlete who helped engineer the escape. Roth (a shortened version of his actual, Polish name) lived in Dayton Ohio, was married, with three children. Max was already living at the Pennington home with his wife and four children of his own. The two men met in Toledo, about halfway between their respective homes. They had an enjoyable time reminiscing about their "bad old days" as concentration camp prisoners, escapees, and survivors.

Some of their death camp brothers and sisters were not so lucky. Numerous friends and relatives perished in the Holocaust. The pair agreed to get together at least once a year, and to this day, Max and Rudy continue to meet and reminisce in Toledo. The last time they met, Max proudly told Rudy that his youngest grandson would soon be a bar mitzvah. Max beamed when delivering the news.

Chapter 4: L'Dor V'Dor—1990

"That's my story, Zachary, and I am sticking to it."

"Oh my God, Zayde. I knew you were a prisoner of war, but... wow... what a story! You should write a book!"

"Many people have stories of bravery during the Holocaust. I am no braver than anyone else. 6,000,000 Jews lost their lives during the war. They are the heroes, my son, not me. I was lucky."

"Some people make their own luck, Zayde! You are one of those. I'm so proud to be your grandson!"

"Then you'll do me a favor?"

"Anything."

"Tell everyone you know about the brave Jews who escaped from Auschwitz, but don't tell them about your grandfather."

"Why not? I'm so proud of you! You were part of the resistance."

"Because it is not important that one of these people is your Zayde. All Jews are relatives—all are important, especially after the death of the 6,000,000 and so many other attempts to wipe us out. Somehow, by the grace of Hashem, we have survived. I don't want you to brag about your Zayde. Use another name when you tell the story. Swear to me and I will give you your Bar Mitzvah present."

"That's blackmail, Zayde!" Zack exclaimed.

"Do you want your present or not?"

"You win, Zayde. What's the present?"

The old man reached behind his head and unlatched his necklace. He reached down the front of his shirt and retrieved a gold pendent that hung from the necklace. It was a large, solid gold Star of David. Max handed the pendent to his grandson.

"Oh my God, Zayde. I can't accept this. Your Zayde gave this to you. You hid it from the Nazis for years. You've told me the story a hundred times! It is precious. You should keep it, Please?"

"L'dor V'dor, my son, from generation to generation. This is Jewish tradition. You've known this since you were a small child. There is a beautiful prayer we sing in Shul. When Hashem gave us the commandments, He wanted us to pass these instructions onto our sons and the sons of our sons. It is our responsibility as Jews to pass traditions on from generation to generation, to keep them alive. I hope you will carry this with you, always, and remember your Zayde and his story of the Shoah."

"I will, Zayde. Thank you, so much, from the bottom of my heart."

"You are welcome, from the bottom of mine. One more thing I must ask of you, Zachary."

"Anything, Zayde, anything."

"Go to school. Make something of yourself. College was not in the cards for me, but it is for you, here in America. Make me proud, do something to help people who are less fortunate. Become a doctor, maybe? My grandson, the doctor. I would be so proud!"

"I don't like science or math, Zayde. And I hate blood. You must like science and math to go to medical school. I will go to college, though. I promise I will do something to help other people. In school last month, I read a wonderful book."

"What book is that, my son?"

"To Kill a Mockingbird" by Harper Lee."

"I have not read this book. What is it about?"

"It's about a lawyer who takes on the case of a black man who is falsely accused of hurting a white woman. The town is racist, and everyone thinks the black guy did it. Everyone, that is, except the lawyer, a guy by the name of Atticus Finch."

"What does this lawyer do?"

"He fights for his client, against everyone in town. Even his own daughter doesn't completely believe the man is innocent."

"What happens?"

"Atticus loses the case. His client, Tom Robinson, the black guy, is found guilty by a white jury. Tom tries to escape from prison and is shot and killed by the guards."

"That's awful, Zachary. This sounds like Auschwitz. Why do you like this book? It sounds terrible."

"Because, Zayde. Atticus tried to help someone less fortunate. He tried, even though the town hated him for it. In the end, most townspeople respected him for what he did. I want to help people who need my help. And I want to help no matter what anyone else says. I want to be a lawyer, Zayde. Will you be proud of me if I become a lawyer, like Atticus Finch?"

"Yes, Zachary, my dear boy. I would be so proud of you if you become a lawyer like Atticus... what's his name?"

"Finch, Zayde."

"Attitus Finch. If you become a lawyer like Atticus Finch, your Zayde will be very proud."

"Can we get desert now, Zayde? Bubbe made her famous apple pie and pie dough cookies."

"I hope there are some left over. We've been here for more than an hour. I'll bet everyone has already eaten dessert."

"Shit!"

"Zachary! Such language!"

"But, I'm a man now, Zayde."

"No reason to curse, young man. Let's have some pie."

Zachary Blake clasped his treasured Bar Mitzvah gift around his neck and followed his grandfather into the dining room. His family had generously left the two 'man-sized' pieces of pie and several cookies. Zack proudly displayed his Jewish Star necklace. For some strange reason, Zack's mother began to cry.

The following morning, the family walked three city blocks to Beth Abraham synagogue. Zachary Blake was the star of the service, a poised young man who studied hard, had a nice voice, and knew his stuff. He chanted his haftorah and some additional maftir parts without error. His young melodic voice boomed to every corner of the shul. After the core service, Zachary chanted the traditional closing prayers, the Ashrei, Aleinu, Ein Keloheinu and, finally, Adon Olam. At the end of the service, he again said the prayer over the wine, and was permitted to take another sip. Zachary Blake had become a man and his parents, Bubbes and Zaydes on both sides of the family were very proud. Zayde Max Lewin and Grampa Morris Blake chanted the Hamotzi over the bread, and the feast was on. What Jewish celebration does not end with feast?

Epilogue: 1991-Present Day

Almost a year to the day after his Bar Mitzvah, Zachary Blake received terrible news. His beloved Zayde, Max Lewin, suffered a heart attack; he was not expected to live through the night. Zack and his family rushed to Zayde's side at Sinai Hospital in Detroit.

Zachary was horrified when he first saw the old man, tubes and machines hooked to every orifice on his body. He looks terrible, the boy heaved. His eyes began to water.

"Come closer, little man," Max beckoned. "I won't bite. All these tubes and machines are scary looking, I know, but they won't hurt you."

Zachary huddled close to his grandfather and burst into tears. "Don't leave me, Zayde. It's too soon. I'm not a lawyer yet," he cried.

"I could have died in the Shoah, my son, but Hashem chose to spare me, so I could live, marry, have your mom, and she could have you. L'Dor v'Dor, Zachary. L'Dor v'Dor.

"From generation to generation, Zayde. I know."

"I do not question His judgment. I am grateful to the Almighty for the time He gave me, a full, rich life I have enjoyed. I am most grateful for my wonderful children and grandchildren. Whether I live or die today,

I know you will honor your promise, become a lawyer, live an honorable life, and help the less fortunate."

"I will Zayde. You know I will."

"Go in peace, my son."

"I love you, Zayde," Zachary cried. "I will never forget you."

"I love you too, my sweet boy. You will only know how much after you have had children and grandchildren of your own."

Fourteen-year-old Zachary Blake kissed his beloved grandfather for the last time. The old man was cold to the touch. This was Zachary's last memory of his grandfather. Max Lewin aka Max Lewenstein from Poland, Holocaust hero and survivor, died in the middle of the night.

****

At his funeral, Max was eulogized as the hero he was, despite his own wishes to the contrary. Young Zachary was powerless to stop those Jewish forces greater than a fourteen-year-old kid. Rudy Roth attended and presented a stirring eulogy, recalling their time together at Auschwitz, the daring escape from the notorious death camp, and yearly get-togethers. After his riveting presentation of the "story", Roth concluded:

"I last saw Max about six months ago in Toledo. How could I know this would be the last time I'd see him or talk with him? We reminisced about 1930s Warsaw, a vibrant and wonderful Jewish community, a time when we proudly exclaimed our Judaism, went to Shul every Saturday, observed Kashrut, celebrated the holidays and the Holy Days, and observed the traditions of our heritage. We spoke of our arrival at Auschwitz, the deplorable conditions, and Max's elaborate escape plan. 'We were crazy, no?' Max recalled." The funeral attendees laughed out loud, long and hard.

"So many were sent to the gas chamber. Without Max and his daring escape, without Max including me in his plans . . ." Roth faltered, paused, and cleared his throat. "I would not be here today. I thank Hashem, every day, for sending me an angel named Max Lewenstein.

As I look out at his wife and beautiful family, his children and grandchildren, remember; you too would not be here today if not for the extraordinary bravery of the angel, Max Lewenstein..."

****

Zachary Blake, Detroit's king of justice, clutched the gold Star of David hanging from his neck. He smiled at the memories of his grandfather, Zayde's wartime heroics, their special conversation, the gift on the eve of Zachary's Bar Mitzvah, his grandfather's dying wish, and Rudy Roth's stirring eulogy. Zachary sat alone in Judge Emma Pearl's courtroom, in Detroit's City County Building, principal home of the Wayne County Circuit Court, a key venue where Zachary Blake plied his trade. He had just completed a major medical malpractice jury trial in front of Judge Pearl, a former litigator in Zack's firm, and one of his favorite judges.

The jury decided in favor of Zack's client in a contentious case where the accused doctor refused to settle the case for any figure, convinced he had done nothing wrong, even though surgery resulted in the client's life-threatening complication. The surgeon and his out-of-town defense expert testified that this complication was an ordinary risk of surgery. Zack's local, far more credible expert testified to multiple breaches of the standard of care. Substantial damages were awarded; the doctor and his insurance company promised an appeal. Such is life in the legal arena— lawyers and clients may not count their chickens until all appeals are hatched.

Still, Zack was satisfied with the outcome. He knew the defense appeal would likely prove unsuccessful. Judge Pearl was a careful jurist; her rulings were rarely overturned on appeal, and this particular trial was error free. An opportunity for substantial defense billings, he ruminated.

Zachary closed his eyes and his thoughts again drifted to the memory of his grandfather's Holocaust heroics. Zack and his wife, Jennifer, often made sizeable donations to the Detroit area Holocaust Museum in Max Lewin's name. Zack provided testimony on Max's behalf, a recorded and detailed account of the story Max shared with his grandson, and a tape of Rudy Roth's stirring eulogy. His grandfather was opposed to personal gratification or reward. Zachary knew this testimony went against the old man's wishes, but this was important. Besides, his parents and Rudy Roth let the cat out of the bag.

Zachary was fully on board. Jewish resistance and prisoner ingenuity were vital parts of Jewish history. The story deserved to be told and Zachary felt a deep personal obligation to tell it in his own words. L'Dor v'Dor, Zayde. He had a duty to report his grandfather's heroic exploits to generations to come.

With some blips on the radar a few years ago, Zachary Blake had fulfilled his promise to his grandfather. He was a lawyer. He won high-profile cases for people who sorely needed victories. He made a fortune in attorney fees from his cases, invested wisely, married the love of his life, and had wonderful children from two marriages. Zayde wouldn't like the fact I divorced, or the fact I married a Schiksa the second time around, but he'd be happy I'm happy.

Zachary Blake was indeed helping people less fortunate, winning their cases against large corporate and insurance interests, donating huge sums of money to social justice causes, and doing so in honor of his late parents and grandparents. Success permitted him to accept only the best cases and, further, allowed him to accept important pro-bono cases. He rose, packed his briefcase, and strolled to the courtroom exit.

"Still here, Zack?" Judge Pearl called from the front of the courtroom. "Nice job for your client on a tough case. Two-week trials are a beast."

"Thanks, Your Honor. You headed out?"

"Yes, but I still have a lot of work to do." She held up her briefcase.

"Me too," he groaned, holding up his own briefcase.

"So, why are you still here?"

"I was sitting at the counsel table, ready to leave, and my thoughts drifted to my grandfather. Today is the 30th anniversary of his death. He's the reason I became a plaintiff's lawyer, you know. He made me promise to help people less fortunate than myself."

"He would be very proud of the man and the lawyer you have become, Zack. We both know it wasn't always that way."

Zachary remembered well an embarrassing incident in Judge Pearl's courtroom during the down years following his divorce and firm break-up.

"Everyone has his or her ups and downs. Thanks to my wife and her fabulous sons, I've more than righted the ship."

"That's a huge understatement, Zachary. It may sound condescending for me to say, but I am proud of you. I know your grandfather would be proud of you too."

"Thank you, Judge; I appreciate it.

"Say, Zack? May I ask a favor? You can say 'no' if you're too busy."

"What is it, Judge?"

"I teach legal advocacy at the University of Detroit, and the class is visiting my courtroom next Monday, for mock trials. Would you mind speaking to them? Perhaps judging one of the cases?"

"I don't mind at all, Judge. Sounds like fun. I'd be honored. In fact, my grandfather would say it's my obligation."

"How so, Zack, if I may ask?"

"L'Dor v'Dor, Your Honor, L'Dor v'Dor."

"Huh?"

"It's a Jewish thing, Your Honor. Don't worry; I'll be there."

The Art of Anticipation
Bianna VanOchten-Joyner

9:30 PM
My hands rest at the bottom of my cold steering wheel,
the rattling sound of the rustic plastic on my '05 Escape
ills the chilled interior.
I bend the curved roads leading to my house,
my arms blanketed in goosebumps,
as I am too excited to even turn the heat on in
October.

My thoughts flashback to that night,
staring at my phone screen,
"Add to Cart",
reflects into my pupils
"65.34",
I spend it,
after weeks of deliberation as to what I really need.

I crookedly park on the street,
walk the swirly path to the back door,
motion-sensored lights illuminating my path.
When I reach the door,
I'm greeted with a package,
Amazon.

My face erupts into a smile,
my feet into a tip-tap happy dance,
and I pick up the box,
and hug it close to my body as I fumble to unlock the
door.

When I reach my bedroom,
I kick off my shoes,
and with each inch of tape that is ripped off,
so is all of the stress that this year has caused me.

In Each Moment, Everything Belongs
Karen Lulich Horwath

"We'll do everything we can to help you as soon as possible," the insurance claim agent tells me on the phone as I watch thick snowflakes fall outside my kitchen window, covering the early spring grass with a unexpected white shroud. "Your adjustor will call you in about an hour, and once he gets to your area, he'll want to meet with you to see the vehicle." The voice on my iPhone speaker is smooth and reassuring. "We're all working from home now, due to the statewide shutdown, so we just ask your patience."

****

In my rearview mirror I see the gas station attendant race out the front door and around the corner to the pump where my car has stalled. The mouth behind his thick dark beard screams at me in a steady staccato of clipped English, the accent tangling his words relentlessly. "You... you break it... my gas pump... you drive zee car... you don't hang zee nozzle... you are thief... you must pay!" His panic is palpable. I stare in disbelief at my gas tank, which has been partially pulled up through the nozzle opening, then pivot around to see the entire front of the gas pump dangling helplessly in a twisted pile of metal hanging around the nozzle like a metal noose. As I bend down to look under my car, it slowly dawns on me that I have pulled away from the gas pump with the nozzle still in my car's tank. I blink the snow out of my eyes as it starts to fall thickly around me.

****

"I found toilet paper!" my daughter tells me on

the phone. "I had to get to the store right when it opened, though, like by 6 A.M. Go early tomorrow." She knows I would prefer to sleep as late as possible, shut out the Coronavirus pandemic that has startled our country, our world, into quarantine, isolation—shutdowns of every school and business hitting like dominoes knocked recklessly against each other too soon, the sound of doors closing clanking all around us, especially in the school where I teach.

****

Walking into the grocery store for the first time in two weeks, I am conscious of each step, each person I pass in the aisles. The cloth mask a friend sewed for me feels foreign on my face, elastic ear loops digging into the soft tissue behind my ears, my breath hot and contained inside the double-layered eight-inch fabric that stretches from the top of my nose down below my chin. My glasses fog up, and I pull the mask up under the bridge of my glasses so that I can see. I spy a four-pack of toilet paper in the carts of four shoppers as they exit the store, and I sigh in relief at the thought of grabbing a pack for myself.

****

My principal interrupts our 2nd hour class over the P.A. Her voice is calm, measured, but insistent. "I need every student and teacher to listen very carefully. Take a moment to stop what you are doing and sit down." She outlines the steps in the governor's order. All schools are closing. All businesses are closing. All public spaces are closing. We are locking down, quarantining, isolating in our own homes for at least two weeks, maybe longer, in an attempt to stop this strange virus that is sickening everyone who inhales infected air. Or touches infected surfaces. "Students, you will be dismissed to clean out your lockers. Take every textbook back to your classrooms, every library book back to the media center, every school instrument back to the band room. Throw out all food, old assignments you don't want. When you are finished, keep your locker open for it to be sanitized." Teachers are similarly told to take home all personal belongings. The principal makes it sound like an adventure – tells students that they will be getting an extra two weeks of spring break. During my morning classes, I assist my 7th graders in their locker clean-outs. In the afternoon, my last three hours are high school classes, and these students help me carry crates of my personal books and desk items to the car. At the last minute, I pack up all my binders of teaching supplies. Something tells me we might be home longer than two weeks.

****

I blink in disbelief as I slowly maneuver my cart through the aisles. At 6:30 A.M., I'm too late for toilet paper. There is one roll of paper towel left on the shelf. But not a single box of Kleenex, pack of toilet paper, or package of napkins remains. As I move through the store, my head turns from empty aisle to empty aisle. The meat counter is empty. The bread aisle is empty. The cereal aisle is empty. There is no rice, flour, quinoa, lentils, or noodles. There is no war, we aren't being bombed, we don't even have to ration supplies so our soldiers can survive overseas. Yet the store shelves are as empty as if our town were under siege, as if every store has been shelled and this is the last one to remain open, intact. I make my way down the canned and frozen food aisles, filling my cart with four of everything. At the end of one aisle I see one remaining industrial-sized bag of rice. I heft that up and plop it into my cart on top of my cans of tuna, corn, tomatoes, and artichoke hearts. The snow is falling as I load my groceries into the car. Two more stops before total quarantine begins: the bank and the gas station.

****

My daughter's graduation for her master's degree program is scheduled for April. As we sit in quarantine, her college announces that there will be no university walking ceremony. Instead, her program will do a one-hour Zoom webinar. Each graduate is able to wear his or her regalia and will be given the opportunity to announce themselves in a two-minute speech. She is devastated. After three years of classes, projects, and seminars—all while working fulltime—she has been looking forward to the graduation stage ceremony as a way to capstone her learning. After a day of sobbing, she finds her own way of celebrating— decorating her cap and gown, taking pictures at iconic university locations, and setting up her own personal Zoom champagne toast after the webinar ceremony is complete.

****

Walking into the automotive shop, I am aware of every step I take toward a person. How far apart we stand. If we breathe in each other's direction. There is no way to know who is sick, who carries this unknown virus, who I should avoid. A small hand-lettered sign sits next to the bottle of hand sanitizer on the counter. As I squeeze the pump handle, the drop of gel feels cool on my palm, and I rub it vigorously over my hands as I hand my insurance paperwork to the station attendant. "I drove away from the gas station with the nozzle still in my gas tank," I tell him. He chuckles: "Not like in the movies, is it?" Good news: there is a junkyard that has a replacement part for my gas tank. It will not cost me $800 after all—just money for the scrap gas intake neck and cap system. The station owner offers to have the body shop across the street do all the pre-fitting work, and we are able to work out a payment schedule once my auto insurance check is delivered. No one laughs at me. And, when I deliver the insurance check, they smile and say thank you.

****

At home, our family creates our own celebratory environment for Valerie's graduation ceremony. We buy a congratulations sign, a bottle of champagne, and use our iPhones to record her short graduation speech. I am surprisingly emotional when her name is announced as having received her master's degree in Educational Leadership: Higher Education Student Affairs. She forms her hands in the shape of a heart, curving fingers together, anchored by touching thumbs. She flashes this heart around the computer screen, beaming. After the event is over, she opens her own Zoom call and dozens of her college friends flood the screen. We all join together to toast her graduation, and she is clearly dazed at the outpouring of support she receives. One friend has dropped off gourmet donuts; another friend has dropped off little gourmet cakes; other friends have delivered champagne to her apartment doorstep. Graduation is a little different, but it is definitely celebrated. As tears threaten to spill, I say goodbye and leave the Zoom call to the young people—for them, this will be their graduation memory.

****

I drive by the service station where I had my accident. The insurance check has been cut, and I see that a new pump cover has replaced the one I destroyed. The black plastic garbage bags that once shrouded the ruined pumps have been removed. Cars are once again lined up for gas.

****

Two days later, my husband walks in the door. He lifts an eight-count roll of two-ply toilet paper above his head. "Victory!" he proclaims.

****

In-person school is cancelled for the remainder of the year. Our district purchases a planned online curriculum, which I supplement with discussion of an online novel about the pandemic, written one chapter a week in real time: Mitch Albom's Human Touch. My students love it.

****

Mother's Day weekend dawns, and the weather is finally warm enough where I can visit my elderly parents and sit outside, six feet apart, for the entire day. I make the two-hour drive on a Sunday, and my daughter plans to meet me there. I have her graduation gift in the back of my car, as well as a gift for my mom, who will turn eighty years old in just a few more months. I arrive first and am just arranging my mom's gift—a large colorful flower arrangement—on a table along her front porch.

As I water the bourgeoning flowers, my daughter pulls up in her car and rushes up the sidewalk. We haven't seen each other since Christmas. I reach out to bump elbows with her—my new pandemic standard greeting—and say, "Elbow hug?" She flings herself into my arms and clasps her hands around the back of my neck. "No, we're hugging," she sobs, folding herself into me the way she did when she was a little child. "This has been so hard. I've missed you so much."

We stand on the sidewalk in front of my parents' house, tucked into each other, her tears melting into my hair, my tears soaking her shirt, time collapsing into every embrace we've ever had. We stand there rocking each other into comfort as the spring sun pulls itself up over the aging maple trees. Their buds unfurl and leaf into fullness, grow green then turn orange and red, then drop as fertilizer into grass, lie barren, bud again—while we stand there, soaking into each other's love.

Fantasy As Medicine
Olivia Duby

I'm accustomed to slamming my feet into the mud beneath my swing set to stop abruptly when I really need to, but that doesn't change the fact that sometimes I stomp down a little too hard and it hurts like hell. Tentatively lifting my foot off the frozen ground, I hissed in pain and yanked my headphones off my ears; I just wanted to go inside, it was damp and a cold out and I'd been swinging for over an hour at this point. Truly, all I was craving was to curl up in bed but what else was there for me today? Or tomorrow, or next week for that matter. Since the beginning of the pandemic, time had slowed to a syrupy crawl and sprang to a lightning speed all at once; everything seemed to blur together—I had no idea what day it was.

I love to be alone, I really do, but too much of anything is just too much. There was an apathy to the circles my thoughts ran in; a lack of care that should have been there. I couldn't bring myself to change out of my pajamas on most days now, it didn't seem worth it. Thus, I made my way through the damp, overgrown grass up to my back porch, lifting my fuzzy pajama pants to keep them dry. Some nerve in the center of my foot seemed to ache from my impulsive stop; there were at least four different dogs barking on my block at the moment. I didn't mean to slam the screen door as loudly as I did; when I heard my mom yell something at me about it from the living room, I figured it must be the weekend in order for her to be home. I rounded the corner and she was sitting in her usual spot, the large red armchair slightly diagonal from the TV; she had on pajamas and was scrolling through her phone. At least I wasn't the only one in a bad mood.

"Sorry, I didn't mean to shut the door so loud." I plopped down on the couch next to her chair and started to remove my many hoodies. Mom raised a brow.

"How many times do I have to tell you to not slam that door? Is it really so difficult?" she replied. We were quiet for a few minutes, conversations didn't seem to really go anywhere these days. Suddenly, she reached for the Roku remote on the table and booted up Viki, which was where we watched any foreign TV shows. Mom sighed.

"I'm out of dramas, I can't find anything on Netflix and the only other thing I'm watching is currently airing," she whined. I looked up from my phone and rolled my eyes.

"Try Hulu," I deadpanned.

She seemed to light up with an idea when she pushed her glasses up and began furiously clicking through her liked shows.

"Watch something with me! We haven't watched anything together since Kingdom, and I have this Chinese fantasy drama saved in my likes but I don't want to watch it alone. I read it's really good! I bet you'll like it, it'll get you out of that room of yours," Mom said.

When the clicking noises ceased, indicating she'd likely landed on the show she was talking about, I reluctantly looked at the TV screen. Upon the screen, in usual Viki fashion, the title of the show sat near the top (with a short synopsis) accompanied by a star rating; to the right was a large piece of promotional art and subtitle settings, towards the bottom, a list of episodes.

The Untamed (9.8 stars)

I studied the promotional art, which depicted the two lead actors (who were quite cute) standing side by side, one holding a black flute with a red tassel hanging off the end up to his lips and the other unsheathing a white sword. Their eyes were closed but they seemed to stare at me. Huh.

"It looks familiar, I think I've seen this on Twitter or something." I looked over at my Mom to see her pulling up a list of the cast on her phone.

"It's very popular, it's been recommended to me several times. You know I tried to watch that Chinese drama with Zhang Yixing in it, and I just couldn't seem to get used to the sound of the language. Maybe if you're giving commentary the whole time, I'll get used to it faster. At least, that's what I'm thinking." Mom started to pull her hair back into a ponytail and snatched a blanket off the back of her chair, preparing for what she hoped to be a binge-session.

I've always been incredibly picky when it comes to television; I can't just commit to however many episodes or seasons unless I'm absolutely sure it's going to be worth it. It's not because I consider my time to be so valuable I wouldn't dare spend it on anything less than Oscar-worthy writing and acting, it's more so because I'm not the type of person who can just stop thinking about a story once it ends. I can hardly fathom what it's like to be able to finish a book or a show and just move on like nothing happened; when the story ends it will stop playing on my TV but that doesn't stop me from thinking about it day and night for weeks on end. Characters don't just pass through my mind, they unpack their things and decide to stay for a while, settling down in my brain.

Ultimately though, what else was I going to

spend my time doing? The overwhelming force of the pandemic was incredible, it had forced life itself to simply halt altogether. I used to spend so much time wishing and praying to any God or being who would listen to me: "Please, I just need a break. Everything is so much right now, I don't want to do this anymore." Now, my prayers had been answered; everything had stopped. I was on break indefinitely, responsible for all of absolutely nothing. I was benefiting from quarantine, but it hurt. It felt like I was capitalizing on the pain of others, and my precious "break" hadn't even been all I'd hoped for.

Suddenly, I felt overwhelmed with the childish desire to get utterly lost in something; the closest thing I'd ever felt to true magic in my life was the sensation of being completely consumed by a world that wasn't my own. I've heard people say escapism is normal and even healthy in small doses, but I don't think I've ever been prone to a healthy amount of escapism; for me it needs to be all or nothing, and whatever story I'm escaping into needs to be perfect. For the first time in a long time, I wanted that so bad it was painful; it had been far too long and I had worried before that I'd grown out of it.

So, maybe the reason The Untamed has 9.8 stars on Viki is because it does that for other people like me. Or maybe, it's just one of those dime-a-dozen fantasy dramas that tend to get popular once in a while. Either way, I was struck with the realization that I had time to kill and no suitable murder weapon. A few episodes couldn't hurt.

"Okay," I said, placing my phone on the table and grabbing a blanket off the back of the couch. "We can check it out."

****

As a result, we watch the first couple episodes and suddenly we're thrust into a romantic world of betrayal, love, and most importantly, tragedy. I would later come to know this genre as Xianxia, which is basically an entire genre based on Taoism and ancient Chinese mythology where through the practice of meditation and magical martial arts, characters can "cultivate" to achieve immortality and get epic powers they use to fight monsters and demons. This may sound ridiculous to some people, but I've always been of the opinion that the best stories use fantastical elements to their advantage. They are also by far the best kind of stories for escapism.

The story follows a young man who rebels against the injustice of his world only to be killed for it and remembered as an evil heretic; he is then resurrected to carry out an act of revenge sixteen years later, which ultimately results in him reuniting with his soulmate, and the two of them go on to uncover years of political corruption as well as unravel the events that surround the main characters death.

Basically, it's the greatest thing I have ever seen and my mom agrees. We end up binging it any chance we get over the next couple of weeks.

By the time we make it to episode twenty, I've taken to sitting down on the couch and waiting for my mom to get home from work during weekdays, anxiously waiting to pick up where we left off. I have something to look forward to. The second I hear the lock on the kitchen door click at quarter to five, I spring into action.

"I've been waiting for you to get home for like an hour! What is taking you so long today?"

"Can I get in the door before you start? Jeez."

My mom sighs and sets down her things on the kitchen counter. "I'd like to change out of my work clothes before we settle down."

"Are you going to make dinner tonight or is Dad? We need to see if Lan Zhan and Wei make up! I don't like that they were fighting last episode…" I whined.

"They'll make up, they have to. Wei is just pushing him away because he wants to protect him," Mom replies.

"I know, but I wish they'd just talk to each other."

We'd continue to chat while Mom bustled around the house putting away her work materials and saying "Hello" to all our pets. Once she was finished with all of that, she'd change into some more comfortable clothes and we'd settle down in the living room to watch The Untamed for hours until our heads hurt from reading subtitles and we'd cried over some event in the show at least once or twice. There was something so grounding about the series; the tale was a simple thing to indulge in and a simple thing to worry about when everything else in the world had never been more complicated. Our days became built around finding time to escape into its world; it was so easy to fall in love with the characters that we fell fast and fell hard.

The storyline of the show was complicated and heavy at times, dealing with dark issues, and the CGI was really kind of awful, but my Mom and I couldn't find it in ourselves to care when everything else seemed so perfect. The story of The Untamed and the novel it's based on can largely be divided into two main sections: everything that happens before Wei Wuxian dies and everything that happens after Wei

Wuxian dies; the show begins during his resurrection and we follow that for two episodes before being thrust into a flashback of his youth and downfall for thirty-one episodes. It creates this wonderful tension towards the end of the flashback because as a viewer, you're waiting for the other shoe to drop; you know something awful is about to happen but can't quite pinpoint what it is. That sort of tension felt all too familiar these days. In episode thirty-one an event occurs that sets every horrible atrocity the flashback has been building up towards into motion, the worst sort of domino effect imaginable; I don't think I'll ever be able to forget the feeling of watching that scene with my mom—we had to pause the show and take a break. Our jaws were actually hanging open in shock.

"...What?" I muttered, a surprised giggle rising in my throat. My mom looked at me with wide eyes.

"Did that really just happen? This changes everything, he can't die!" she said.

"Oh my God, this is the thing that gets Wei killed, isn't it?" I laughed in disbelief.

"I'm usually pretty good at predicting plot twists, but I would have never seen a death like that coming! Oh my God…" Mom replied, equally shaken. We sat there with the show paused in silence for a moment, trying to process what had just happened. What was there to say? Suddenly, there was excitement and fear for what was to come and we needed to tell somebody; we ran to the basement where Dad was watching Star Trek: The Next Generation.

"Dad! You won't believe what just happened in our show!" I shouted. He looked up from his own TV screen, unimpressed with our explosive bewilderment. My mom and I went on to explain that this character had been killed and for all intents and purposes it looked like the main character had done it and how that was going to give all the people who were against him the excuse they needed to attack him mercilessly; how his soulmate would definitely stand by his side but it wouldn't be enough and he would die tragically, ripped from the arms of the man he loved. My dad nodded along with our explanation but seemed relatively uninterested, when we were done with our spiel he answered simply: "Wow, that's crazy."

Similar things occurred throughout the rest of our first viewing of The Untamed, but eventually after many more episodes and scenes that left us in tears, the show that had been our rock finally came to an end. A few minutes after the credits of episode fifty rolled, we scrolled back as far as we could and clicked again on episode one.

****

About a week or so after we began our second viewing of the series, my mom and I reached one of our favorite arcs in the show, one where our characters get trapped in a cave with a giant turtle-snake monster they were forced to fight by the evil Wen Clan. It's a lot more lighthearted than other portions of the show and so it serves as a nice break from some of the more emotionally charged episodes. When we were watching the sequence where the characters begin to descend into Xuanwu Cave, my younger brother Jackson happened to be walking past the living room.

"Tell me you're not seriously watching this again? I'm so sick of hearing about it from you guys." He groaned and moved to enter the kitchen.

"Why don't you watch this episode with us? The next fight scene is really cool," my mom said.

"Leave him out of this, he's a party-pooper, he'll ruin it for us," I said bitterly.

"Shut up, I'm not a party-pooper," Jackson mumbled.

"You might like it," my mom said and patted the ottoman in front of her chair, signaling him to sit down. He sighed and submitted to our mom's pleas, plopping down on the ottoman with his arms crossed. We watched for about the next twenty minutes before my brother declared: "This is gay."

"Jackson—" Mom began. I cut her off.

"Maybe it's because the main couple is two men, you dolt," I said bluntly.

"That's not what I meant, shut up," Jackson answered.

"Fine. I wouldn't expect you to understand something as sophisticated and intellectual as The Untamed. It's far too highbrow for you; go play Smash Brothers or something, you idiot." My mom sighed at our bickering, while my brother turned his nose up at the TV and walked away.

****

The next time Mom and I finished watching all fifty episodes of The Untamed was around May, and we were determined to force Dad and Jackson to participate in the third viewing with us. The show just seemed to get better as we watched it more, we noticed new things every time. We ordered take out so no one had to worry about cooking dinner and announced to the boys that they would be watching at least the first three episodes whether they liked it or not. Once we had retrieved our food and dragged everyone from their respective corners of the house into the living room, we all settled into our normal spots on the couches and chairs before booting up the TV and finding episode one. Things were going relatively well for the first few minutes, Mom and I glued to the screen as always, but my Dad was barely paying attention and my brother would simply not stop asking questions.

"If his name is Wei Wuxian, why are people calling him Young Master Mo?" he asked.

"Because he got resurrected into the body of a guy named Mo Xuanyu," I'd replied.

"What's a cultivator?"

"Like, someone who does magic and has a golden core."

"So, why did this guy Jiang Cheng kill Wei?"

"Jiang Cheng didn't kill—" I started.

"Goodness gracious, could you two please just watch the show and be quiet! I'm trying to listen! Jackson, you'll find out everything if you just pay attention!" Mom snapped. We both stopped talking and sunk down into the couch. By the time episode two was over, Dad and Jackson were both incredibly confused but also intrigued by the plot; after all The Untamed is quite unlike any other show we'd watched as a family up until this point. Mom and I turned to look at the two of them, brimming with hope that we might get to share our new favorite thing with the whole family.

"Do you like it?" we both asked. Their response was lukewarm, but they said they were intrigued enough to keep watching into the flashback sequence. It was a small victory, but a victory nonetheless; the two of us desperately wanted to share the thing that had brought us so much joy during the pandemic with others. So we kept watching; it took Dad a lot longer to become invested in the story than it took Jackson, who, after getting over the fact that The Untamed is "gay" was completely hooked into the story. Now, he was one of us; so, all we had left to do was to get Dad into the show which we figured would happen on its own as the story naturally gained momentum. He became much more interested in the story as Wei Wuxian deviated from the path of orthodoxy and became the Yiling Patriarch, because that really is the section that shines the brightest. When we reached episode thirty-one, he was flabbergasted at the plot twist.

"Are you kidding me!? This is going to ruin everything for Wei, and he's done nothing wrong! How could they just kill that character!?" Dad exclaimed. Jackson was quiet with shock after the scene; Mom and I were laughing uncontrollably, the kind of laughter that comes so powerful and quick you can't breathe and your stomach cramps up.

"That's what we were trying to tell you about that one day in the basement!" I giggled, practically keeling over from amusement. Jackson seemed to be finally processing the situation.

"But... they'll blame Wei for it and he'll have no way to deny it," Jackson said. Mom tucked a curl behind her ear.

"Well, I guess you'll just have to wait and see what happens."

****

When it was finally over (a third time for Mom and me even though it was only the first time for Dad and Jackson) we were emotionally exhausted; somehow, the adventure seemed much more overwhelming with everyone watching. We would pause the show to talk and make jokes; during the day my brother and I would text each other about it even though in reality we could just walk across the house and talk in real life. The pandemic had made things different; some of us were desperate for conversation and human interaction while the way others coped with the situation was by withdrawing further into themselves. I was definitely doing the latter; it was easier for me to do what I always did when I was upset, which was to go to my room and read or play video games until I was tired enough to take a nap. That worked on days when I only had a bit of free time but was then expected to get up and resume my schoolwork or other responsibilities; now though, I had free time all the time and I couldn't just keep playing the same video games and reading the same books for weeks on end.

Luckily, my mind never seemed to tire of the world of The Untamed. It helped that it was endlessly popular in certain online circles, so there was always fan art to look at and fanfiction to read; discussions were always being had about this character or that scene, what one piece of dialogue meant or even the symbolism found in the detail on characters' clothing. It was an endless waterfall of escapism that I was all too happy to drink from. Of course, I also read the original novel after finding an English translation of it; I also watched the donghua, read the manhua, and listened to the audio drama versions of the story. I felt so spoiled by this one series, connected to it in a way I hadn't been able to connect to a story since I was much younger. I'd always been able to use escapism but I hadn't been this consumed by something in a long while; it was euphoric, addicting.

My family and I watched the series another time after our third watch because Mom and I convinced Dad and Jackson the show is better the second time around, and we couldn't just let them watch it without us, now could we? Then that re-watch came and went, the withdrawal was powerful but we were able to cope for a few weeks before giving up and clicking on episode one again, a fifth time for Mom and I and a third time for Dad and Jackson; eventually that viewing ended as well. Now it has been many months since my Mom and I first started watching The Untamed, falling deeply into the romantic and tragic world of Wei Wuxian and Lan Wangji. Still, I'm deeply engrossed in this alternate world. The pandemic is "over", yet it really isn't. We've all been thrust back into day-to-day life despite the fact that there is no vaccine and we're arguably less safe than we were in March. I'm back in school, well, mostly. It's easier to go outside now though; as the election approaches there is more hope for relief from this strange situation. The seasons came and went even though my daily routine didn't change with them; the ground beneath my swing turned from soft mud to nearly dry as concrete before freezing once more. These days when I go out there to ground myself sometimes I listen to The Untamed original sound track and it calms me enough to prevent me from slamming my sneakers into the dirt. Life has become a sort of fog or state of limbo; a small sense of normalcy has returned to me but I find myself searching in the dark for my old world. Still, I can't let the story go; the characters sit with me every day and I wonder if this tale will stay even when I don't need its presence anymore.

The Life of The Old Oak from Brockway
Christina Inman

The three-hundred-year-old oak tree made its home in the middle of my driveway. He reached up, racing against skyscrapers, trying to be bigger and bolder than they were. He loomed over the ancient house that was almost as old as the oak. Throughout time he whispered stories into the wind of the things he had seen since he was born. The old oak spun tales about the time he was struck by lightning but stood strong and stayed for over a hundred more years. Storms were no match for the mighty oak; he overcame all storms no matter how treacherous.

Old oak saw many owners and ended up watching my family and me grow up. We walked by him every day on our way to school and when we went to play outside. He smiled and posed in our pictures when family was over and when we went to dances.

Oak housed so many creatures; a baby raccoon sat two stories up while old oak watched us jump at the sight. He gave shelter to a family of groundhogs, who lived in the hole in his trunk. The ants and squirrels were constant guests, but the oak didn't care—he loved seeing animals enjoy the home he made for them.

He gave us shade during the scorching summer and sheltered us during the rainy and snowy days. He played pranks of falling over by dropping branches in the grass to remind us that he was there, but we never forgot. We admired him for living so long and being so strong, but we watched as he grew old, slowly weakening day by day.

The pandemic quarantine took a toll on his heart; the old, mighty oak was slowing down. He didn't see us leave the house for three months besides to get groceries. Our isolation hurt old oak's heart, and he wanted to see us enjoying the warm days again.

Then he decided to make the biggest sacrifice; on one particularly windy day, he decided that we should be outside more. That is the day he fell. He chose to fall into the grass so we wouldn't get hurt, but so we would have a reason to go outside.

This three-hundred-year-old tree gave us purpose in times of confusion and chose our happiness over his own. He lived longer than we ever will, but to give old oak's death purpose, he fell so we could survive.

Gratitude for Sports
Noah Birnbaum

March 12, 2020. The day that the sports world came to a dead stop. Athletes told to stay at home. Student athletes had the news broken to them that there will be no spring sports. With sports completely gone, I realized what joy I got from watching and playing.

May 17, 2020. The first day racing was back I cried tears of happiness even though I was not a big racing guy.

March 18-July 22, 2020. WIth no major sports to follow and races only once a week I sat in front of a boring television screen anticipating the day for a major sport to return. Constantly looking for updates on seasons for any sport that will restart soon.

July 23, 2020. Baseball is back. My favorite sport is finally back and I could not be more ecstatic. Baseball being gone just made me love it even more when it came back.

July 30-August 1, 2020- Basketball and hockey return. Now with three of the four major sports in America back, my entertainment is slowly coming back. Still not being able to see them in person, I cheered from my couch in my air-conditioned house.

Now the NFL is back on time and college football is back after a slight delay. Sports may not be the same as they were before March 12 but I sure am glad that they're back. Now when I sit down to watch a sports game with my dad, I take a minute to appreciate it.

Dependence
Robert Bond

Since we don't have a usable garage, the leftover fireworks from last year sat in the foyer indefinitely. Every once in a while, my younger, pre-teenaged brother, obsessed with things that go boom, would ask my dad if we could light a couple off, even if it wasn't the 4th of July yet. Dad always had the same answer: "not tonight Shaunce, I have work in the morning," to which my brother would frown and shuffle off to find some other thing to break.

I was usually in the living room when he asked, playing some video game alone or with a friend, sitting on a chair taller than the couches for a better view of the TV. It had been dragged in from the dining room across the house and never got put back. From where I sat, I had a direct view of the fireworks—sticking their heads out of their cardboard box home, begging to be shot into the night sky. Every time I saw that Shaunce was going to ask my dad about them, I slipped off the right side of my gaming headset. "Not tonight, Shaunce," was all I needed to hear. I slipped the headset back in place.

As the year went on and COVID-19 got more serious, social life began shutting itself down, much like the stores and businesses in my city. Face mask recommendations became "must have face covering to enter" signs; stay-at-home options became stay-at-home orders.

I remember waking up on March 13th to the news that school would be canceled for a couple weeks, and while that might make someone out there worried, I was nothing less than ecstatic. Two weeks of no school, right into another week of spring break? It was as if someone took all the snow days that we wished we had earlier in the winter and lined them up for us now.

Back then it was still only recommended that we stay home, so of course I spent almost every hour of every day at my girlfriend's house with her and her family instead of my own. But that freedom came to an end pretty soon, as Michigan's stay-at-home order was issued and a few free weeks at home turned into a few boring months.

So much time in the house without being able to go see a movie or hang out with friends forced everyone to get creative in ways to entertain themselves. Friendships and relationships were put to the test, and while some proved how strong they really were, others showed that long distance doesn't work for them. Over time, I traded in my best IRL (in real life) friends for my good online friends, my girlfriend and her family for my family and our next-door neighbors.

I grew more acquainted with the fireworks and their cardboard box from my seat in the living room. The big green mortar always hid itself behind the smaller boxes of multi-colored sparklers; the flashing strobe lights mixed in with the little smoke bombs, whose long fuses coiled themselves around the edges of the main box; the ripped open packs of firecrackers littered the floor of the container.

Days of the week blurred together into long, seemingly endless streaks of boredom, until the only thing keeping me sane was my dining room chair in the middle of the living room with my PS4 controller in my hand.

After asking so many times and getting the same answer, I think Shaunce just gave up on the fireworks.

Eventually he stopped asking, and so they just continued to sit there. Every day, as the 4th got closer, the fuses on each one seemed to grow a little longer and the head of each rocket seemed to get a little taller, but they sat there nevertheless, waiting for Independence Day to come.

Even though my family spent more time than ever under one roof, we all still stayed in our own general areas at first, secluded from each other. Shaunce spent his time in the basement with our dog, chasing him around the pool table and knocking things onto the carpet until they were both sprawled out on the ground out of breath. My slightly younger sister Shayla stayed in her room doing Lord knows what in day-long group calls with her friends. Every once in a while I'd hear a shriek of laughter, which let me know she was still alive. Even my older sister Rainah came home for a while since her college campus switched to finishing out the semester online. It was nice for her to be around more, but she was mostly focused on school and her boyfriend, who spent his time on her phone screen since he was stuck back in his hometown. Mom's job was one that could still be done from home, so most days she sat in her work space from the time she woke up to the time she went to bed. Dad's job, on the other hand, couldn't be done from home, so instead of being in the loud, stressing, automotive plant all day, he loved to be in his natural habitat: outside on the front porch. With the living room being the center of the house, I witnessed bits of everything—bangs and barks beneath me, shrieks and laughter behind me, parts of a conversation happening all around me—but I had no one to really talk to.

The 4th of July is meant to be a day of pride for this country, but my family just uses it as an excuse to meet up with our cousins, aunts, and uncles. Every year we get together with fireworks of our own, eating and laughing before heading out in about nine different cars to see the city-wide lights show. But this year was different. This year there was no get-together, no food, no show.

I woke up that morning and went straight to my usual gaming spot, assuming there would be no celebration because there was no one to celebrate with. Mom still had to work, and Dad didn't tell me he had any plans, so I sat there, roaming the virtual world of God of War until the daylight ran out.

Just when it got really dark and I was starting to lose interest in playing anymore, I faintly heard a voice call my name from far away. It was Shayla, who I didn't even realize had left her room, calling me from the back door of the house a few rooms away.

"R.J!" she shouted.

I slipped my headset off my ears. "Yeah," I replied, "what's up?"

"Dad said come on outside with me, him and Shaunce."

I didn't really want to join them. Laying down in my room sounded better.

"And bring the fireworks."

While playing the game inside, I hadn't realized how much celebrating the rest of the city was actually doing. People all around the neighborhood had their own mini fireworks shows going on, no different from what normally happens when people went home after the big show, except now, everyone was doing it.

My younger siblings and I took turns lighting the big fireworks, admiring each and every sparkler, every firecracker, and every smoke bomb. Lighting the big green mortar in the street of my front yard made me smile harder than any other thing this year. It shot up from the base with a PFFF and smacked the sky with a POW, much louder than any of us expected. When it exploded, I felt a thump in my chest, followed by the warm sensation of satisfaction.

When we ran out of fireworks and were gathered around the porch, Dad brought out his big speaker and put on some music for us to vibe to. We all knew that if anything could bring the Bond family together, it would be late 90s/early 2000s R&B. As soon as Ice Cube's "Today Was A Good Day" came on, the environment evolved from a listening session to a dancing party.

Mom could feel us moving the house she was trying to work in, and after being stuck in her office for so long, she just said, "forget it," and joined us outside. Rainah told her boyfriend she would call him back later, uniting the household for the first time in months. There was no coordinated movement, no pre-planned style of dance, we just got up and moved, singing "shake 'em up, shake 'em up, shake 'em up, shake 'em" in unison for the whole block to hear. We recreated moves we saw other people do to Outkast's Hey Ya! and belted out the duo lyrics to Jill Scott's So In Love With You for the audience of our neighbors. We even had a small, six-person conga line jumping to some Hispanic song I didn't even know.

After weeks and weeks of sitting down and sitting back, we couldn't help but feel the need to be active. "I'll take this as my prom replacement," I jokingly told them as we tried to finish doing the Biker Shuffle.

With the street light at the end of our driveway being the only source of light around, our silhouettes danced away the tragedies of the world around us. For hours, it seemed like we were the only people on the planet. No virus, no phones, no thinking—just music.

Just a family, from dusk till dawn.

Death or Magic
A. Kidd

Is it death or is it magic
that stops pollution for a day?
Germs are swimming thriving
traveling by air
as we stop flight
stay home and talk to each other for once

Taking a break is winter
spring is the birth of so much agony
We spring forth
they leap into our open mouths
We are tigers preyed upon
by the tiniest of adversaries,
an enemy of us all—
That which doesn't kill us
humbles us
United under the stars
but forced to pray alone,
faces frozen to our phones
Ironically that's where most germs reside

We want to hide out under masks,
buy all the water that could feed
a million starving children overseas,
rub ourselves raw with alcohol—
Fear forces us into corners, under blankets, into closets
but is it death or is it magic
when the magnolia blooms early anyway
and so many have already survived.
Governments are pooling resources
businesses are waiving fees
wine is flowing instead of water
we're protecting one and other
Death is a common threat

which causes social distancing
but meanwhile children are magic:
laughing, dancing, growing wild
Their little hands still touching everything
until we teach them to
disconnect—

Even if we can't hold hands,
we can hold hearts—
be not only vigilant
but hold vigil
hold someone else's gaze long enough
to see commonality
Humanity
Community
Unity
We can see magic in the deadliest of threats
if we try

The Most Peaceful Place Ever
Andrew Allen Smith

Dee watched out the car window as the trees barreled past the window. As she turned and looked forward the road seemed to ease on forever in front of them with no end in sight. The fresh black asphalt could have been poured minutes ago and the deep ebon path was a start contrast to the endless layers of pine, maple, birch, and oak grasping at them from everywhere. Max, the Jack Russell Terrier, sat on her lap.

"It's grown up a lot since last year," Dee said to her husband Karl.

Dee and Karl Dreamer were a matched from the perspective of the world. Karl was a successful businessman in plastics and textiles. His shrewd negotiations and progressive view of the industry had allowed him to create a small but profitable company where others had barely begun understanding the market. The spooled threads of 3D printers were mixed, matched, boxed and sold at an amazing rate as the world become more and more dependent on 3D printing and his company, Michigan Dreamers had vaulted to the top as they released more colors and finishes to a nascent market.

Dee was successful in her own right. Gifted with a knack for public speaking she had gained notoriety and a fair following speaking to writers and future writers on the craft, and had written a series of books herself. Although Dee and Karl were not spring chickens, they had only married a few years ago. Sometimes it took time to find the right person, and they both professed to everyone they just found the right time.

This was a time they looked forward to each year. A getaway that was both relaxing and extraordinary. Years ago, they had purchased property in the Grayling area. Twenty acres of rustic land in the middle of nowhere jutted up against public land in the Huron National Forest. The combination of the small plot of land against the much larger state park gave them a solitude and isolation only a few could understand. They choose many weekends to visit during the year to unwind, and one special three-week vacation to be alone and apart from the world.

This year they had timed their three-week getaway with Election Day. The mounting tensions of political strife had been a strain on the world, and the incessant drone of political ads on every media type spraying insensitivity and negativity had made them decide months ago that near election they needed to be away from it all. As the election approached it only got worse and they knew they had made the right decision.

"Yeah," Karl smiled at his wife, "too much rain, not here we are in revenge of the weeds. Sounds like one of your stories huh?"

Dee laughed, he was always trying to make her smile, "It will give me something to write about."

"Now, now," Karl chided, "You are mine for part of this trip, can't just write all the time."

"You know I can," Dee shot back, "Writing pays the bills too."

Karl nodded, then pouted a little, "but but but, your husband needs you."

"Season starts this week, you know I will be out there with you in that blind."

"You better be," Karl laughed. "We may have to live off the land if the election goes wrong."

"I'm not so sure which wrong is wrong anymore. Voting for the less wrong, wrong still seems wrong."

"Are you singing a vote somebody wrong song?" Karl giggled.

"God, what a dad joke," Dee said. "Where do you come up with these."

The car was slowing down, and Karl turned onto a gravel road. The road had been graded sometime recently and was not the bumpy mess it usually was when they came up. Still they both started humming and the noises were like singing in a fan over and over as the bumps vibrated their bodies like a chair in the center of a mall.

"Twenty minutes of this, I may need new fillings," Karl laughed.

"It's worth it," Dee giggled as she bounced a little on a deeper bump. "This Ursa and Major will be around this year?"

Ursa and Major were a pair of bears that roamed the woods near their property. When they first got the property, Dee wanted to sleep outside but Karl advised against it. As she pushed back Karl pulled out his phone and showed her the footage from the trailcams and Dee saw the two bears wandering together, eating and playing like massive children in the woods outside their cabin. Dee had said, "Oh, I get it" and they laughed about it often now. As the years had progressed the bears were a common sight and they had learned to just leave each other alone. Black bears are not aggressive usually, and Ursa and Major had come close to the house only to seemingly nod and leave when spotted.

"Who knows," Karl said, "I didn't have a cell number to let them know we were coming."

"Oh, they know," Dee said. "They always seem to know. Millie might be back; we will have to watch out while Max is out."

Millie was the name they had given to an elusive bobcat they had seen only a few times. With the park so close to their property it was normal to see a lot of animals, and Karl and Dee respected them. Though they hunted they ate what they killed, though they lived on the land, they lived with the land at their cabin and respected the animals as the primary residents. Their caution had allowed them to avoid being sprayed by skunk, quilled by porcupines, and attacked by various coyotes and other animals. Last year they had heard a wolf sing in the night, but when they called the DNR they were told it must have been a coyote, and there were no wolves in the lower peninsula. Still, it gave Dee food for her books.

They continued to drive, and the forest grasped at them and the road got more bumpy. Karl slowed as he always did so their Jeep Cherokee would survive the constant jarring. The SUV was an amazing piece of equipment, but Michigan potholes often swallowed Volkswagens and a good pothole could take a tire off if taken too fast.

As they rounded yet another curve they came to a blocked road. It happened from time to time as jack pines split at the top and fell in the wind. They were not heavy trees, but it was better to get it out of the way rather than risk having it caught up in the truck. Putting the truck in park the two got out and walked to the branches.

The two put on thick gloves and Dee grabbed several of the shattered sticks and started throwing them to the side of the road. Her short blonde hair whipped in the wind as Karl grabbed a larger branch and started dragging the severed treetop. Dee went to help and started pulling on another branch and it moved much faster. The branch, weak from years of dry decay snapped and Dee fell backwards and landed on her bottom. The momentum and reset of force broke Karl's branch and he bumbled down next to her.

"Well that went well," Karl laughed. "We can get around though."

"My butt hurts," Dee said as she stood.

As they reached the car, they looked out in the now clear dirt road. there, before them, stood a Grey Wolf. The wolf stared at them both and shifted its olive-green eyes back and forth. It advanced two steps, stopped and peered into their eyes.

"No wolves in the Lower huh?" Karl said.

Max barked inside the car as he looked out. The small Jack Russell was noisy, but the wolf looked to be well over a hundred pounds and did not even flinch as Max challenged.

Karl opened the car door and as he got in the car Max tried to get out. Karl grabbed him and put him in the back seat. The wolf did not move. "Max, you need to quiet down before you become dinner."

Dee had gotten in the other door and closed it and as they started the Jeep. Again, the wolf did not move it stared directly at them with its piercing eyes, holding, challenging but not aggressive at all. "What is going on here, is something trying to keep us from getting to the cabin?"

Karl stared forward; the wolf stared back. Karl put the car in gear and slowly moved forward. The wolf continued to stare, and then, without warning, bolted into the thick woods.

"Wow, just wow," Dee said, "Once in a lifetime."

"Did you get a picture?" Karl asked.

"Damn, why didn't you say something." Dee was exasperated. "I mean, we knew it was a wolf and were told no way. This would have been pure gold."

"It was pure gold," Karl said as the SUV slowly moved forward. The wolf was gone, deep in the woods with no trace they could see.

The two were quiet for a short time as they continued driving and then turned down an even smaller dirt road. The road was even worse, but it was the last leg and their ten mile per hour drive was a known entity and relished more than disliked. A few minutes passed and they saw the edge of the cabin. Smoke was coming from the chimney and they were a little concerned.

Karl stopped the SUV and looked at Max and Dee. Max was excited as usual and ready to run the woods while Dee shared his concern. They usually saw no people here, and liked it that way. They had no indoor toilet, and the outhouse ran off people who normally would be rushing to bother them. The solitude was not something most people would seek out and they had never had anyone squat on their property.

"Stay here?" Karl asked.

"Hell no!" Dee said as she opened her door and got out, making sure the small dog stayed in the Jeep.

They walked to the door and noted it had been forced. Karl pushed open the door, "Hello!" He said in a low shout. "Who is here? You are trespassing."

"Is that so," came the voice behind them.

Dee and Karl turned to see a man with a shotgun pointed at them.

"Nice Remington," Karl said, "Who are you?"

"I was about to ask you the same thing." the man said. "You said I am trespassing?"

"Yeah," Dee said, "This is our cabin, and you need to leave."

"Seein' as how I got the gun, I think I make the rules," the man said as he pointed the weapon at Dee.

Dee stepped back a short step.

"No no no," the man said, "don't be moving. You need to stay still until I figure out what to do with you."

"Do with us?" Karl said, "You should leave, we have people coming and all of them will be armed." The last part was a white lie, there might be people coming and they might be armed but the man didn't know that.

"Well thanks for letting me know," the man said, "I was only planning on staying the night, but maybe if I get enough of you I could stay longer."

"Why are you here?" Dee asked. "This is our house."

"Right now, it is mine, and I'm meeting up with some people further on to visit the National Guard base up the road a piece. We are gonna be ready for this election whichever way it turns out."

Another voice from inside the house said, "Glen, why'd ya have to go and say that?"

"You said my name," Glen shouted as a second man with a Henry rifle appeared.

"Glen, Glen, Glen," the man repeated. Do you know how many Glens there are in Michigan? Who cares? Still you told them where we are going so now we will have to tie them up or kill them before we go."

"You callin' me stupid?" Glen asked.

"I didn't say a word. Just that you shouldn't have done that," the man replied.

"Look folks," the man said, "Sure, this may be your land, but right now it is ours, well, mine. We are staying the night and then we will tie you up and move on. If you decide to be a pain in my side, we will just kill you. Ain't no big deal." The man looked up, "The sun is going down now and in a short time it will be dark. We should get unpacked and inside for the night, and then this will be over. Glenn, watch them unload the car then get some rope so we can sleep for the night."

"OK Sam," Glenn said with a lot of emphasis on Sam's name.

Sam laughed and sat down on a chair near the door. "What are your names?"

"I'm Karl and this is Dee." Karl said. Dee looked at him with a little anger. "What?" Karl said, "Would rather be Karl than hey you."

Sam laughed a little, "Well Karl and Dee, unload your car and get in here. Gonna be a long night."

They walked to the Jeep with Glen right behind them and opened the door. Max jumped out and barked. Dee tried to get him, but he stayed elusive and as Glen became more frustrated, he fired a shot in the air. Max ran from the loud noise and was in the woods in a second. Dee started to chase, and Sam yelled, "No, let it go. The dog is on its own."

Dee looked at Karl, he nodded, and the two grabbed a few boxes and walked them to the house. It took fifteen minutes to unload and Glen checked everything. He was going to take the bows and two rifles, but Sam said no to leave them in the car, take the keys, lock it, then throw the keys in the woods. "Never take a man's gun. They can find the keys when they get loose, we will be long gone."

"But is it a nice shotgun Sam," Glen had said, "Real nice."

Sam had laughed and said, "You can't be seen with a nice gun, what would people think." Glen had swung at him for that, but missed and Sam just laughed. "Tie them up for the night and we will be out of here in the morning."

Glen was good at knots and binding people up. The two were tied up on the small couch and their bonds were comfortable but quite tight. There would be no getting out.

Outside the skies with crimson and pink and faded slowly to a violet then darkness was upon them. From inside the cabin it was still light from the fire in the fireplace and the windows were lit up with the moon and stars. Time passed and soon it was midnight. Dee and Karl had listened to ranting and raving all night, mostly from Glen, who was ready to get some army stuff and take on the world. The two discussed odd items as well, from women in the movies to the latest pistols and a few other items.

As midnight passed Glen was rummaging through boxes and pulled out books that Dee had brought. He looked at the back and then looked at Dee. "Hey this is you."

"Yeah, so?" Dee snapped.

"You famous?" Glen asked, "Like ransom famous?"

"No," Dee said looking down, "I wish. You might get a dollar ninety from a few people I know."

"Know anybody famous?" Glen pressed.

"A few people," Dee said, "Writing is for entertaining people, fame does not play into it."

"Sounds like something a famous person would say," Glen said.

"Leave 'em alone and get some sleep," Sam barked, "We have to get up before first light."

The two men lay down, and Dee and Karl looked on.

"How are we going to get out of here," Dee whispered.

"Working on it," Karl said as he moved ever so slightly.

They both continued to quietly struggle against their bonds to no avail for nearly an hour as their captors slept.

Some things are hard to describe. The sound that rung out has been defined by Stanley P. Young as "a dozen railroad whistles, braid them together, and then let one strand after another drop off, the last peal so frightfully piercing as to go through your heart and soul". It rung through the cabin and the two men jumped up right away.

"What was that?" Glen said.

"Wolf," Dee stated.

"There ain't no wolves around here, just in the UPers." Glen shouted.

"We saw it on the way here," Dee smiled. "It is a wolf, and where there's one there's more."

Glen grabbed his gun and stood up, "there is about not to be." he said and ran to the door.

"Stop," Sam said. "Just sit down, we are inside, it is outside."

"But Sam," Glen said, "If its a wolf we gotta get

back to the car and well, it might get us."

"If it is a wolf, and I doubt it is, it is more afraid of us than you are of it," Sam laughed.

"I don't know Sam, I don't like wolves, or even Coyotes." Glen said as he walked back to his sleeping bag and sat down.

"Just get some sleep, we will leave in a few hours," Sam said as he added a log to the fire then walked back to his sleeping bag.

The howling stopped and they heard the loud chuff of a big animal. Glen jumped up again. "What's that?"

"Probably the bears," Karl said.

"Bears? We have Wolves and Bears?" Glen panicked. "We should go Sam."

"Yer an idiot. Haven't you ever spent a night in the woods?" Sam growls.

"Not with wolves and bears," Glen replied.

"Go to sleep," Sam said.

It was only a few minutes there was even more noise outside, the *yip yip yip* of Coyotes filled the air, birds chirped in a panicked frenzy of sound. There were other sounds that were near deafening and Karl and Dee looked at each other. "This is new." Dee said.

"New," Glen was a mess, he was sweating, sweating a lot. "This is not good. Sam, we need to go. I don't care who wins the election, I want my bed back and my house where there are no wolves and bears and all this stuff."

"God you are a baby," Sam laughed. "Got sleep in the truck."

"Alone?" Glen said. "No way."

"Then shut up and sleep," Sam said and lay back down.

Dee looked at Karl as the outdoor symphony continued, "Max?"

"He will be fine," Karl whispered. "He will hide 'til morning."

The sounds were near overwhelming, and Glen was shaking like a mouse waiting for a snake to pounce on him. He held his shotgun like a close friend and looked from window to window to door.

Then Sam sat up as the wolf howled again. The sound was unique and both beautiful and terrifying. The sounds stopped. It was quiet.

People don't understand how quiet it is in the woods. The trees and leave absorb sound, and pine trees break it up even further. In the fall and winter, the sound is so quiet you can hear a pin drop. The eerie silence continued, and Glen was even more agitated.

There was a scratch at the door. Glen swung his weapon to the door and fired several times. The door gaped open, a large hole in it.

Sam yelled, "Idiot. I am deaf now." It was true, the indoor blast of the shotgun had all of them wondering where the phone was ringing as their ears suffered from the loud blast.

"I wanna go Sam," Glen said, "I wanna go now."

The silence continued outside. Sam walked to

the door and looked out, there was nothing there. Whatever made the scratching was gone.

"Get your stuff," Sam said. "Let's get out of here."

Glen packed his backpack so fast it looked like a cartoon. In a matter of moments, he was ready to go. Sam was slower and Glen paced like an expectant mother waiting for a husband to get the car after her water broke. As Sam finished, he looked at Dee and Karl. "I don't wanna hurt you, but you need to give us time to get out of here. You stay put for an hour or so, then I am sure you can find a knife and saw your way out."

Dee looked at him, seething. "Well thanks for visiting my house, how about you stay away next time."

"Don't you worry about it," Sam said, "You won't see us again."

Karl poked Dee as she started to say something, and she stayed silent.

The men left. Dee and Karl were alone.

"Our door," Dee said.

"There is another one in the shed, remember." Karl replied. The sounds began again. Louder this time. "We need to get out of these ropes."

"They said to wait," Dee replied.

"Let's not," Karl said and stood and shimmied to the counter. He turned, pulled out a drawer, and with the tips of his fingers pulled out a knife.

"How are you going to do that?" Dee asked.

"I'm not, you are," Karl said, shimmied back to

her and turn around. "Grab the knife and saw my ropes."

In twenty minutes, they were free. There was no cell service in the area, but they did have a radio. They turned it on and put it on channel 19 and called for help. In a few minutes the State Police answered. It was a weak signal, but they got the message.

Karl and Dee went outside, and the noises were overwhelming, but as they stepped out the normalcy returned. There was a rustling in the bushes, then Max ran and jumped in Dee's arms.

Dee hugged the dog, and they went inside and waited. An hour later a trooper pulled up with his light on. He knocked on the door and as Dee and Karl answered he was examining the hole in the door.

"Dee and Karl Dreamer?" the Trooper asked.

"Yes," Dee replied as she looked at the tall man in his crisp uniform and perfectly shined shoes.

"We caught the men you described. Their truck was broken down, a tree had fallen and they tried to go over it. Either of you hurt?" He asked.

"No," Dee said, "Just glad to be alive and free now."

"The two men were ranting and raving about being attacked. They kept saying wolves blocked the road. Then they said a bear tried to get in their truck, and their doors were pretty scratched up."

"Crazy people huh?" Dee said, "There are no wolves in the lower peninsula."

The trooper nodded. "I need to fill out a report."

Thirty minutes later the trooper left. Karl hammered a piece of wood over the door and they made the beds. "I'll replace the door in the morning," he said.

"I guess I have lots to write," Dee replied, "while you do that door."

"Did you plan this so you could write?" Karl chided.

"Umm, no," Dee laughed rubbing her wrists, "But it is a good story."

At 4 AM they laid down with Max on the bed and soon fell asleep holding each other tightly. Outside the woods watched over them and the night faded into day in the most peaceful place ever.

Stay Home, Stay Safe
Jared Morningstar

The gas tank's been full for weeks
because there is nowhere to go:
restaurants are as empty
as toilet paper store aisles,
hotel rooms get as much use as
the Bibles in their bedside drawers,
and the neon city lights
that used to beckon lonely men
to come inside, to forget their pain,
no longer shine.

Stay Home, Stay Safe, they say,
or the plague outside will get you.
It is the end of the world to many.

But I feel fine.

For safety to me is
the twinkle in my daughter's eyes,
her smile
as we stumble our way
through making pizza together,
her laughter
while making me look like a fool
during games of Uno and Battleship,
and every hug she gives me
before going to bed.
It's my son's unlimited happiness
every single time he learns
how to read a new word,
when the rain stops
and we can finally take that walk,
or at the end of a long day
when all he wants to do

is watch The Cat in the Hat
and cuddle on the couch
with big, goofy me.

And it's singing Jason Isbell songs
together with my wife,
talking about those vacations
we'll take one day,
and sitting on the porch years from now
watching our grandchildren play,
and holding hands the same way we did
before the virus:
the same way we will
when it is finally gone.

Life isn't always predictable,
and it surely isn't always
milk and honey,
but I am forever grateful,
for when I am home,
with love all around me,
I will always be safe.

Clarity
Lily Miller

The world fell into a chaotic silence, deafening and sharp, like jagged walls closing in around my body as I fell to my knees. The world looked like the obscure designs that only appear on the back of my eyelids after they have been closed for far too long. Shapes I have never seen before in the dimmest colors that no mixing of lackluster paints could recreate. When the pandemic hit, I rocked back and forth in the new world that seemed to be stuck underwater until I found a shell that, when pressed against my ear, amplified the ambient noise of the ocean we were drowning in. Until that, I could only hold my own hands against my chest so I knew I was still warm.

That silence was so immensely cold but became my common companion.
The Earth was giving off ragged breaths that my ears strained to make sense of, to prove its existence.
Its true and golden existence.

When the world first shut down, that very silence was deafening and overwhelming. It went quiet so quickly, and all I had left were my thoughts because the world could only offer me questions. That shell brought me out from under the surface of the water. I could plant my hands in the grass and dig my hands in so deep that the dirt would pill under my fingernails and in the crease of my hands to show me I was still here. Here, with my shell pressed tightly to my ear, so I knew that the silence was not a mistake.

As soon as I knew that silence and I were meant to be, we became inseparable. The shell never left my ear. The questions continued even as the bitter weather of March, there when this all started, disappeared. The world faded into summer weather, and my ocean in my shell came even closer. My golden silence melted in between my fingers and became mine, dissolving the dirt under my nails. The virus still burned hot as well—unappeased by no man or vaccine. Silence and I didn't care. We never left the house.

I fell slowly in love with the clarity silence brought to me, even as questions of the world began to be published in the papers, questions of a vaccine, and a new world. I no longer sought them out, and even as school became closed for even longer, the ocean began to move even closer into my shell. My brain used to be as wild as this sickness, burning with that hot fever. And while that has not slowed down, silence and I cannot be separated.

> *Without the pandemic that created the new deafening silence the world holds,*
> *I would have never found my clarity.*
> *I would still be looking for so many answers.*

The world was forced into isolation when everyone least expected it; when I least expected it. The year 2020 was supposed to be full of prosperity and booming ideas. Yet everything came to a halt so quickly. What once caused panic attacks, rocking back and forth on my floor, has produced a new level of understanding. Silence and I, we were always meant to be.

Queer Confession #2
Donny Winter

I always dreamed of simple things
because the reality of them
seemed too far away, spaced by distance,
years in wait, and a thirst to belong
like a rogue planet lost between
solar systems.

I always dreamed of simple things
and the reality of them seems near
since the universe projected me
forward to now, as he lays next to me
falling asleep still clutching his book,
glasses crooked on his face.

I always dreamed of simple things
and now they're here, tangibly present,
even as I smile, remove his glasses, and
turn off the lamp, I know we burn
like binary stars in elliptical consistency,
So, as I go to bed next to you,

I draw the lines between our eyes
to connect the dots we make in
this constellation, now
refined.

From Emma's COVID Diary
Emma Palova

I kept a diary during the COVID-19 quarantine in Michigan writing daily for forty-six consecutive days. I wrote most of my posts on mom's iPad sitting in a car watching the gray waters of Murray Lake in Grattan Township.

It was very cold on Friday March 13th as we were rushed out of the Devos Hall from the Women's Expo in Grand Rapids as everything was shut down shortly after noon on Friday. That was my first and only live in person author's event of 2020. My last live fan was a pretty woman well-dressed sporting a beige woolen poncho. And the last author I've seen live was Robert Muladore, a veteran of twenty-five years serving with the Michigan State Police. We shared the same table. After shaking hands with a fan, Muladore wearing only a blue T-shirt ran off to the sanitizer dispenser by the wall in the back. The Red Cross was drawing blood next to us in the surreal irony of things to come.

"They're shutting the show down," yelled a vendor handing out flyers for health products.

I called my friends, whom I have handed free tickets for the show, warning them not to come. Disappointment ruled and rolled over us.

Chaos and panic ensued as everyone was trying to escape the huge hall dragging their carts with prized possessions. We had to wait for the industrial elevators to get to the underground parking garage. The parking attendant refused to refund my parking ticket for three days of the show that never happened. I got lost in a city that I knew so well.

When I got home, I started journaling because I wanted to make sure this all wasn't just a bad dream.

The quarantine started on March 23.

Day 11: First walk to the Franciscans on April 3

The nature oblivious to the Coronavirus horrors was waking up from its winter's sleep.

I enjoyed nature's gifts during my first walk to the Franciscan Life Process Center: daffodils getting ready to burst open, birds singing and frogs croaking in the swamp off the gravel road.

Just under two miles, the walk covers a variety of terrain and vegetation enhanced by the beautiful landscape at the Franciscan campus outside of Lowell.

The ornamental grasses were neatly trimmed and the colors of the meadow were changing from yellowish to green. I walked past the vacant parking lot to the St. Mary's Rosary Walk.

On normal days, the center is busy with arts and music programming. People from far and near enjoy the Franciscans' offerings: everything from painting au plain air, music instruction, community gardening, trails to retreats in the yurts or the San Pietro house.

The gardening team is usually busy with their landscaping tasks.

But today it was quiet as the silence pierced my ears and only an occasional robin broke the spell.

I spent some quiet time at St. Mary's Piazza as one of the sisters, who was walking her mutt Pico, greeted me.

"What a beautiful day," she said.

"Yes, it's gorgeous."

At that moment I realized how fortunate we were to enjoy the beautiful Friday afternoon far away from the nation's Coronavirus hot spots.

"What is your name?" the sister asked.

"I am Emma," I answered. "And yours?"

"I am sister Mary Paula," she said.

There has never been a need for social distancing outside the buildings at the center surrounded by open space. I walked the way of the cross several times and I have never encountered a single soul. The same goes for the trails on the 230-acre campus, where you immerse yourself in serenity.

When I got home, my husband Ludek was cleaning up around the outdoors furnace after a long winter.

"Let's go somewhere, it's Friday afternoon," I said.

"There's nowhere to go," he said.

There is still nature left and its bountiful gifts for us to enjoy in the times of the Coronavirus.

Tips: Consider the COVID-19 quarantine as your personal retreat away from the society's hustle and bustle. Let it transform you.

Call and Response
Sam Barbee

Easter Sunrise Service
God's Acre, Moravian Cemetery

A brass band seeps dirges.
Evergreens appease the tomb.
Static cherubs murmur dark syllables
about the timbre of weak wings.
Attuned to grief's chorus, forsaken
hymns suffer in minor keys.

I overhear their impulsive whispers,
morose silence abridged in this
negative space. Quixotic soldier,
I contest their off-key staccatos,
dispute sad shifts into black refrains. . . .
all to summon my lover's sweet call,

and synch her angelic lyrics... empower
songs from divine places where
fertile responds to festive. Delight
conquers with upbeat harmonies,
prompts major chords, enchanting
cantos illuminating slanted dusk.

Her reprise enchants, phrase by phrase,
note by note, incanting only verses that serve.
Melancholy slain, I swerve from solitude's
blight into communal tongues,
transforming chaos into eloquence,
decrescendo into psalm.

That Duck
L.E. Goldtree

I was settin' out on the dock the other day watchin' some folks fishing and some ducks here and there when I heard, 'How you doin'?' I turned to see who it was and nobody was there. Bout when I thought I was crazy, I heard it again, 'Hey, how you doin'? Look down here.'

I looked off in the water and there set a mallard duck. Nothing else. Just a duck. Then I did think I was crazy when that duck said, 'What ya so stunned fer?'

Well. Well is all I know to say.

I mustered up something in me and said, 'you talkin' to me?'

And that duck said, 'You lookin' at me?'

I said, 'You lookin' at me?'

And that duck said, 'You don't believe me?'

Well. Well is all I know to say.

Little time passed by and I just kept staring at that mallard Duck. Wonderinn' what on earth? Didn't have to wait too long until, 'You remember back when your boy was about four or five-year-old? He asked ya if God could tawk to yawl like yawl tawked to him when ye prayed?'

My heart was getting heavy as I began to remember.

'He told **you** God told **him** you were like a duck, but you wouldn't come in to eat crackers with the rest. You was too busy doing tryin' ta do everything by yourself all alone.'

And then the duck said, 'Remember how you cried and held him close to you because you knew he was right. God had tawked to that boy and only in a child's words could such a thing be shown through a story using a 'duck'.

And, then the duck said, 'I have to go now. I see my Drake a 'yonder.

And I watched her swim away.

Well. Well I'm glad I went out on the dock today. Blessed to remember what I forgot to remember.

Ducks 'pair' up. Two is better than one. They are loyal to one another for life. They are loyal to their 'flock'. They fly in a V line working as both leaders and followers. You'll hear them call out to one another as if to say 'Go! You can do this!' as they work off one another's drag in flight and rotate in and out so that no 'one' has to work harder than another.

It's okay to ask for help. Everyone needs someone.

Once again, God has talked and used a 'duck'. *smiles

Boys on the Couch
J.R. Roper

As soon as school was closed and the fear of COVID-19 sunk in, our boys began a nightly migration downstairs after midnight, often interrupting an important rerun of the Great British Baking Show (There is no finer isolation tolerating show on Netflix. That's a fact). It was a strange phenomenon. The boys couldn't articulate why they had to come downstairs and sleep on the couches, and until the stay home and sleep on the couch order, they had never behaved in this way. Was it fear? Anxiety? A need for comfort?

I recall a dream from my senior year of high school right after the attack on September 11, 2001. People were storming our house and just as they entered my room, I woke up. It was vivid. Terrifying. For a while, it made the prospect of going to sleep far scarier than falling asleep in class the next day. Were my own boys having a similar response to the foggy present and uncertain future? Whatever the reason, our little people needed to be close to us.

We tried hugs to keep them in their beds. Then came bribery. Then we made threats. Then our grinchy hearts grew five sizes, and we made a major change. The room upstairs became a bunkhouse for the kids, and everyone was on the same level of the house.

We went to bed that night expecting to find them curled up on the couches the following morning. With just a short hallway separating us, the boys slept soundly that night and have ever since. Living in isolation during the COVID-19 pandemic presented many challenges (and may again still) but the closeness of family overpowered all the fear and anxiety and worry that shadowed the world. We took more walks, had fun pulling weeds (pulling weeds!), and spent more time enjoying home-baked goods than ever before.

The sad and difficult stories of 2020 will forever be in our memories, but in the end, we always find exactly what we are looking for in the world. We can reframe our experiences and interrupt our negative internal software if we so choose. It was a time of isolation from the world. But a time of togetherness with the people I love most. It was a time snuggled on the couch by day and asleep near to one another at night.

As the world tries to return to normal and we all go our separate ways during the day, I miss my family more than ever.

Out of Caution, Abundance
Ray Lacina

You live in days like
some old movie
starring Charleston Heston
you damn dirty ape
and you peek out the curtains
every day a little more surprised
the risen dead don't stalk the streets
maniacs in leather don't ride monster truck steeds
in search of gas
and gas is cheap
but there's nowhere to go
so you lay out Monopoly you
give the kitchen another good clean you
lift your phone and read this poem
grunt your distaste
scroll on.

And if it all feels a little fruitless
because there was no fruit
the last time you shopped
as your hair grows shaggy as your pajamas
wear thin
think of yourself like this, if it helps:
think of yourself
as a vector victor
and each day you're holed up
from the empty streets
fugitive from the day-to-day

is a day you don't catch sick
a day you don't shed sick
and maybe you'd be fine
I pray that you'd be fine
but maybe where you would go
death would trail behind.

From this caution, abundance flows
the mother saved the father saved
the generations blossoming from them saved
the cure for cancer saved maybe the world's perfect
poem
saved maybe
the woman who rushes back into the fire to save
a baby a grandmother a cat
saved
the man who settles on the park bench in dappled sun
breaths deep
and watches a cardinal fly, saved
and in this silence, in this pause
you can perhaps with a breath, with a pen
with a late-night talk, after the kids have slept
have finally slept
you can just maybe rediscover
the who you are without the busy
you can rediscover maybe
your heart
and where it directs you
and if you follow, sitting in your backyard in your
kitchen
in the tiny corner you've made for prayer
if you follow where it leads you'll maybe just find
fervent and fertile and green green green
abundance.

Isolationship
Belinda Subraman

Nearly a thousand died today in the USA
of the novel coronavirus.
I push myself to do the solitary walk outside
as my husband is not well enough to accompany me.
I've made a thick green womb
around a tree
in my backyard garden
I can no longer buy plants, pots or dirt
but I can split profuse aloe vera
and it likes stretching out
filling in new places it is welcome.
An aloe finger offers itself
from an elevated perch
next to my outdoor chair.
It actually curves on the end
as if it wants to be held.
I clasp its cool finger
and feel comfort
and connection to life.
Isolated in quarantine
I take comfort where I can.
I have a husband, two cats
and plants who love me.

Under the Mask
Jason O'Toole

I'm an elder advocate and many of my clients have been isolated and alone well before COVID caused all of us to alter our lifestyles. As an essential worker, I am sometimes the only face they'll see that's not on TV. To keep both of us safe during in-person visits, I wear a KN95 mask which obscures everything under my eyes.

On a recent visit to check on the welfare of an elder, I sensed that she was scared of me. I tried to assure her that I was only there to check up on her and was not there to take her out of her home. She wore a paper mask of her own and above it, her eyes brimmed with tears.

I decided to describe what she could not see. "Ma'am, you can't tell, but I'm happy to see that you're doing well. Under this mask, I'm smiling for you."

The elder paused and her eyes met mine. Her voice brightened as she said "And I'm...smiling... too!"

Once A Stranger
Ja'Niya Howard

There's this unforgettable feeling when a stranger's soul binds with yours through foreign eyes

Ginger hair that resembles Autumn leaves paired with an extra set of eyes enclosed in silver steel

Those undiscovered orbs lay atop a binding layer of hospital-blue fabric that screams "protection"

Her kindness wrapped in a silky voice and ears created for patience

Anonymous barriers and the time and place break down

To you, I no longer feel a stranger, but two people who have met

And grief is handled with warmth

A smile made a home across my cheeks for hours to pass

Just like a glistening penny dives into the dark depths of a wishing well to find the plethora of riches

My heart expands and into it flows the tiniest memory of her light

And there she resides until we meet again

Then Came A Pandemic
D.A. Reed

Well. I never thought COVID-19, quarantine, shelter in place, and social distancing would become part of my everyday language. Then came 2020.

In the middle of February 2020, my family was so busy I remember thinking, "Man, I wish things would just slow down," then looking at the calendar and how packed the next several weeks were. And I felt defeated, to a certain extent.

Then came a pandemic.

There were many people affected more negatively by the virus and shelter in place order from the Governor than my family, and my heart aches for them. It also aches for those who were sick or who lost a loved one due to COVID-19. But trust me when I say I struggled a lot during the time of isolation, and like a lot of people I felt the pressure to be productive during the stay at home order. But I am here to tell you – it was okay not to be productive during the stay at home order.

It's okay to rest, it's okay to immerse yourself in a book for hours on end, it's okay to play basketball with your kids seven times a day, it's okay to take ten walks a day and literally bask in the sunshine and literally smell the roses. Let me repeat: It is okay to rest!

So many of our lives are dictated by strict

schedules and events that keep coming at us without stopping. We feel harried and stressed and just wish for a chance to REST (myself included!). Well, that chance was handed to us. Most definitely not in the way we would have hoped, but 2020 was our chance to rejuvenate our bodies and minds.

I worked to be grateful for the silver linings that continually nudged their way into my consciousness: time to write, the fact my children saw their father every day for two weeks - which doesn't always happen, time to read to my heart's content, the fact that I could say, "Yes, let's do that!" every time my children asked if we could go for a walk or play basketball instead of saying, "We don't have time."

Were there struggles about finances and with family – because (let's face it) you were around your family 24/7 (as much as we love them...)? Yes. Was there still an underlying concern when we had to make that needed trip to the grocery store and be around other people? Yes. Did we still worry for our friends and family who have essential jobs? Yes.

The first half of the year 2020 was a frustrating time, but it was also a time filled with blessings if we were willing to look for them.
Did I still write? Oh, yes. Because I love it dearly. But I did not stress myself out about being productive, or about churning out 'X' amount of stories or books during the stay at home order. I enjoyed spending that time with my children and husband, I reveled in not having a tight schedule we were fighting to meet each day...

I might struggle with what has been "taken away" during this year, but I am so very thankful for what has been "given" to us during as well. I choose to REST. Who's with me??

www.ingramcontent.com/pod-product-compliance
Lightning Source LLC
Chambersburg PA
CBHW071350170626
46811CB00003B/1081